Love in the Key of Summer

Love in the Key of Summer

A Love Set in Summer novel (Book 1)

Zariah L. Banks

Chapter 1
Tawni

Steam curled around us like hookah smoke at a grown folks' house party. Tiff, Trish, and I called ourselves Triple Threat—T-name besties, soul-tied and synced up like three tight strands in fresh box braids. We were sitting in a small, dimly lit room, draped in plush robes. Our legs were splayed over yoni steam chairs like queens on thrones. None of us had ever done this before, but after a brutal Cleveland winter, we were open to any activity that promised rejuvenation.

"Why does this shit feel mildly illegal?" Trish breathed out, her head flopped back against the cushion.

"Because this level of relaxation should be a crime," I murmured, eyes halfway closed. "Y'all... this might be the best impulse buy I've ever made. No notes."

Tiff snorted. "You said that about hot yoga."

"And I stand by it," I replied, grinning. "But this here feels like flipping an inner switch from winter funk to summer goddess."

"Speaking of hot," Trish said, fanning herself with her spa

pamphlet. "Anybody else feeling like this yoni steam is slow-roasting your chocha?"

"Hang in there, bitch," Tiff said. "No pain, no gain."

Trish leaned over her armrest. "Speaking of a pain... in the ass, did y'all hear about who got engaged?"

Tiff perked up. "No, do spill."

"Dante," Trish said, raising an eyebrow at me.

I let out a dry laugh. "Oh girl, I heard about that shit. Good for him. I hope she enjoys emotional immaturity served with a side of overcompensating and seafood buffet coupons."

"Tawni!" they both said in unison, cracking up.

"Seriously, I'm good," I said, waving my hand. "Things ended between us exactly when they needed to. I'm pouring all the time I used to spend on that dying relationship into myself."

"You've been glowing with your whole chest lately," Tiff said, sitting up a little. "Like... actually glowing. I see you putting all that energy back into *you*."

"Exactly," I nodded. "This summer, I'm reclaiming my peace. No lesson plans, no behavior charts, no sniffly noses asking for tissue and Band-Aids every five minutes. Just vibes."

Trish chuckled. "Look, I know you love your students, but I also know how hard you ride for those kids. You deserve this time."

"I do," I said softly.

"I'm just glad we're all finally on the same page," Tiff added. "It's been forever since I've seen this much of you broads."

"For real," Trish agreed. "Let's not let the good energy die. Next month—what's the move? Scenic train wine tour? Toronto?"

"What about the Cleveland Music Festival next weekend?" Tiff asked. "It's supposed to be even bigger than last year. DJ Luxx is hosting, soul food trucks, live music..."

Trish shrugged. "Could be epic."

"It's on the books, then," I said. "Here's to a summer to remember."

We clinked our champagne glasses and drank deep. After a few moments of contemplative silence passed, I exhaled. "Now, help me off this thing before they try to serve my cooked yoni with a side of jasmine rice."

***

Several hours later, his soft and deliberate knock stirred me from my thoughts. I walked down the hallway of my townhome, barefoot, and clutching a throw blanket. Taking a deep breath, I opened the door without a word.

Dante emerged from the late evening's shadow and stepped into my home like he belonged. Like I hadn't just found out from *my friend* that he was engaged to another woman.

His designer cologne trailed him as he dropped his keys into the ceramic dish by the door and assessed me with his signature cocky ease. I pursed my lips and let the silence stretch between us, long and uncomfortable. After letting his lustful eyes slide all over my body, he stepped out of his shoes and started his familiar path toward the couch.

"Nah, we're not doing that tonight," I said.

Dante paused, half-turning. "Alright... then what's up?"

"Were you ever going to tell me?"

"Tell you what?"

I remained standing, pulling the blanket tighter across my chest. "That you're engaged."

After a slow blink and an even slower nod, he said, "Yeah. I didn't mention that?"

"Seems you left out that small detail while blowing my back out, Dante."

His brows pinched, just slightly. "Tawni…"

"You've been sleeping with me for a whole year. And at no point during your whole-ass double life did you think I deserved the courtesy of knowing you were seriously dating someone?"

He scrubbed a hand over his jaw. "It's not like you didn't want it. You're the one sending those drunk texts, inviting me over in the middle of the night."

I crossed my arms. "Yes. I invited you over here, but we had an understanding. Once either of us got involved with someone else, we'd cut all ties… for good."

"Those were your rules."

"Which you *agreed* to."

He took a breath and sat on the edge of the couch, his elbows resting on his knees. "We weren't in a relationship anymore, Tee. You made it clear from the start—no more strings and no expectations. I guess that was at the forefront of my mind."

I blinked. "So honesty just went out the window for you? You were ready to get it in just now, knowing you're planning to get married."

No answer for that. After a few long moments of silence, he asked, "So, how did you find out?"

I folded my arms. "Trish still talks to your boy, Julius, and we both know he can't hold water. Do you know how humiliating that was to find out from my closest friend?"

"I meant to tell you. I didn't want it to happen like this," he said. "Things got serious fast. She's not like—"

"Don't." I said, shooting him a warning glare. "Don't you dare compare us or make this about that."

Dante nodded slowly. "You're right."

I leaned against the living room wall, arms braced beside me, trying to stay grounded. "You humiliated me in front of our friends. Tried to parade me around like I was a prize you hadn't even earned. And somehow, I've still let you have my body all this time like all I went through meant nothing."

"It didn't mean 'nothing,'" he said, standing. "Not to me."

I didn't move. "Then why did it always feel like I was the only one trying to protect me?"

He slowly approached me, but didn't get too close. "I'm sorry, Tee. I can admit that I took what you gave and never asked what it cost you. But you need to admit that I wasn't the only one with walls up. You shut me out long before things got bad between us."

I finally looked at him. "I had to protect myself, Dante. You were reckless as fuck with my heart. You demanded a version of me I couldn't give you. I wasn't interested in the limelight, being at your side like some pretty little prop. And when I stopped molding myself to fit, you laughed with your boys about how I wasn't built for this life."

It was just a suspicion on my end, but instead of denying it, he dropped his head and nodded.

"I tried to convince myself that keeping things casual was safer," I spoke quietly. "That I could separate emotions from sex. For a while, it worked. I only saw you as a means to an end."

I glanced at him just in time to catch the hurt in his eyes. I didn't expect to find that, but I continued. "But when I found out you were planning to spend your life with someone else, it still felt like the joke was on me."

"Tee, the plan was never to hurt you," he began.

"No, of course not. But it was the result, nonetheless." I exhaled slowly, feeling the weight of my next words settle in my chest. "I just want to thank you for this. The apology, the honesty—it mattered more than I expected. Now here's my truth. For a long time, I convinced myself I misread everything.

That I was too sensitive. Too complicated. Too much of something and not enough of whatever you needed. But I wasn't crazy. You made me feel small... and I let you."

He opened his mouth, maybe to object or defend—but I raised a hand. "I'm not saying that to punish you. I need to hear myself admit it out loud. As of today, I'm no longer holding space for the old versions of either of us. Goodbye, Dante."

He watched me, his eyes softening with regret. Then he gave a slow nod and grabbed his keys.

At the door, he turned back one last time. "Again, I'm sorry, Tee. Not just for sneaking around while I was planning a whole new life without telling you. But for how I handled everything. How I handled you."

He scratched the back of his neck, the words stalling behind clenched teeth. "I... didn't protect you when I should've. I know that now. Hell, I knew it then, but I didn't want to admit it. You were always solid, you know? Like, stronger than me in ways I couldn't name. And that made me feel like I had to level the field somehow."

I felt my jaw tighten, but I didn't respond. Just stared at a spot on the wall behind him because looking into his eyes while hearing him finally hold himself accountable after all these years might've cracked me.

He shifted his weight. "I thought pushing you out there more, making us look good, all that—was gonna make up for how small I felt. Like if people saw us together, I'd finally look like the man I was trying to be. I guess it wasn't about you. It was about me having something to prove, I guess."

His voice cracked a little. "I should've told you when I got serious with her. I know that. But I just couldn't close that door. Not completely. Even if I couldn't give you what you needed, I still—shit—I still felt better with you around. You still felt like home."

I glanced at him, nodding for him to continue.

He took a breath, shaking his head. "I was pretending I could have both lives. I showed up in your life when it suited me and was still trying to build another one somewhere else."

He looked broken in that moment, which was new for me. Hearing these words from him was all new for me.

"I didn't know how much I was still asking you to carry. I was just trying to feel whole," he said. "But I realize I was dragging you through my confusion just so I wouldn't have to sit in that shit alone."

He looked like he wanted to say more but couldn't find the words. He nodded, then walked out my front door. His words hung in the air like the Sativa I'd smelled on him. I guess it was his truth serum.

I didn't protect you when I should've.

That line struck me the hardest. Because I now had confirmation that he'd intentionally made me feel small. He'd known how I felt and had chosen his ego anyway.

I expected to feel hollow or angry, but I felt quite the opposite. Dante had been in my mirror for too long—reflecting the parts of myself I needed to fix but didn't know how. But I could finally look forward because I wasn't chasing closure. I'd just received it, and it was mine to keep.

I remained standing in my foyer, allowing the silence to stretch around me like a warm blanket. The apology and the confrontation had cracked something open. Not in a bad way, but in a way that made space.

"I truly hope she brings out the best in you. And that you choose to be better to her than you were to me," I whispered, swiping a stubborn tear as it fell down my cheek.

I heard his engine start. He pulled off seconds later.

I finally moved to the living room and sank onto the couch,

with my elbows on my knees and my head in my hands. I breathed.

Then I stood, walked into my bedroom, and pulled open the closet door. Pushing aside a stack of scarves and shoeboxes, I reached into the very back. Hidden behind an old makeup kit I hadn't touched in years was a small decorative box. Sponge-Bob's wide grin greeted me from the lid—an old inside joke from a birthday gift Tiff had once given me.

I carried it to my bed and lifted the lid. Inside were faded disposable camera prints with timestamps in the corner and worn photos printed from my phone during my early twenties. Photos of college friends, old coworkers, my mom cheesing hard at our family reunion before she started feeling insecure about her teeth. I flipped through them slowly, smiling and nodding while enjoying tender moments frozen in time.

And then I saw us. Me and Dante, at the lake that first summer we began dating. My head thrown back in laughter, his hand resting on my waist protectively. Or was it possessively? Another shot: the two of us in the kitchen at his mother's housewarming party, cheek to cheek, looking in love. And the last one: him holding my hand across the restaurant table while I smiled at the camera, unaware that he was studying me instead. What I used to think was admiration in his eyes now looked like assessment.

I'd held on to those pictures longer than I meant to. I stood, crossed the room, and fed each photo into the shredder beside my desk. One by one. Mechanically but purposefully. With an immense sense of release. When the last sliver curled into the bin below, I walked into the bathroom and stepped into the shower. I let the water run hotter than usual and didn't think about Dante again.

***

Two days later, I was running errands—picking up groceries, grabbing last-minute items for my next DIY project, and stopping at the bookstore for books that would soon find their permanent hold on my nightstand TBR list—when my phone rang. I didn't recognize the number but answered anyway, pushing my shopping cart outside.

"Hello?"

"Tawni, it's Lenora."

Oh no.

Lenora was my supervisor at the Twinsburg school district and only called when she needed something. We usually communicated by email, so a call meant it was something urgent.

"Hi, Lenora. Everything okay?"

She sighed on the other end. "Well... not exactly. I hate to do this to you..."

Then don't. Dammit, don't, Lenora.

"... but Cedric had to have emergency dental surgery. He's going to be out for a few weeks, and we need someone to cover his summer school class."

Cedric had sent me a late text the previous night and I'd been meaning to read it and respond. I sighed, pulling my cart over in the parking lot and nearly collapsing against someone's minivan. "Lenora..."

"I know, I know," she said quickly. "You were looking forward to your break. And believe me, if I had *anyone* else to ask, I'd call them first. But you're the only person I trust who knows Cedric's students and can step in to prevent a huge setback in their progress."

I pinched the bridge of my nose. "How long are we talking?"

"Three weeks, four tops. Part-time. Just mornings, Monday through Thursday."

I closed my eyes. That helped. A little.

"And it's mostly review and enrichment," she added. "Nothing heavy. You'd be walking out by noon every day."

Even though the arrangement was a lot better than I expected, I still paused. This summer was going to be my chance to let my hair down and focus on myself. So much for a summer to remember.

I scooped up my bags and pressed the unlock button on my key fob. "I can't believe I'm saying this, but okay. I'll do it. But only because Cedric is a friend and I know it's truly an emergency. He hates missing time with his students."

Lenora released a long exhale. "Thank you, Tawni. I knew I could count on you."

That was the thing. Everyone could count on me. Even when I needed to count on myself first. After we hung up, I started my car and immediately blasted the AC. My summer wasn't ruined. But it was certainly starting on a different note than I'd planned. Still, I couldn't help but smile. I would get to see some of my favorite students, and Cedric could put his mind at ease while he focused on recovering. Besides, I knew he'd do the same for me.

Just as I was about to back out of my parking space, my phone dinged with a notification from IG.

There was Dante. Smiling on a boat, his fiancée tucked into his side with the lit skyline behind them. The caption read: *"Real love softens you. Humbles you. Finds you when you're finally ready."*

I let out a quiet laugh through my nose. Of course he chose to post this now. Not last week. Not yesterday. But now—after our talk. After he got to lay his burdens down at my feet and walk away with a clean conscience. Now, he could post pictures of her.

I stared at the photo a little longer. The dig was subtle, and it failed to land. It only provided more clarity. Calmly, I hit unfollow, then block.

He could have his version of 'real love.' Because I knew mine was waiting as well. Along with a better version of myself. This summer, I was dead set on finding out exactly who she was.

Chapter 2
Rudolph

I usually experienced my deepest moments of clarity in a cloud of smoke. Sitting in an intimate cigar lounge with the fellas was one of my favorite pastimes. Khamari crooned an R&B tune from the Bluetooth speaker behind the bar, creating a smooth, soulful vibe. I settled into the high-backed leather chair, welcoming the soft buzz as it descended on me. This was my time, and I was looking forward to relaxing and catching up with my boys.

"'Bout damn time you showed up, bruh," Marcus said, puffing on a Maduro and tilting his glass of cognac toward me. "We were about to send out a search party for your ass."

Laughter rippled around our circle. I chuckled while raising my glass of whiskey neat in return. "Man, I told y'all I was coming. Just had to get Cameron squared away with his tutor first."

"How are you holding up with Cam's tutoring schedule on top of everything else?" Kenny asked, his eyes fixed on me.

I shook my head. "It's not easy. But we're figuring it out."

"Tutoring in the summer? Let my man Cam breathe. He'll be alright for a few months," Link said.

I smirked. "Nah, he asked to keep it going. He's been focused on getting into a prestigious high school, so it's all part of the plan."

"Focused, huh?" Link said, shaking his head. "When I was his age, I was trying to sneak into Keisha's house—not into more school."

"It's a different world now," I shrugged. "He's got his eye on that STEM academy, and I'm not about to be the reason he misses it."

Kenny gave a low whistle. "Man. Willow would've loved that."

I didn't respond right away, just nodded slowly and took another sip of my drink. The memory of my late wife often showed up without warning, sometimes like a calming warm breeze and other times like torrential rain. Tonight, I was grateful for her gentle breeze.

"Glad you made time for us, though," Marcus had a booming voice, always the loudest of the bunch. But tonight, it was settling. "To celebrate, we'll let you pick up tonight's tab."

We laughed again, easing me into the comfort of our usual banter, like old times. We talked sports, relationships, and brotherhood, along with the usual trash about who was too old to come hoop on the basketball court, who needed to stop lying about being in the gym before hitting the basketball court, and who was most likely to need a life flight to the ICU from the basketball court.

"So, how's business been, Rue?" Kenny asked, exhaling a billow of smoke.

I exhaled, leaning back. Work was the last thing I wanted to discuss. As a project manager at a bustling construction firm, the demands never seemed to relent.

"Nonstop, man," I said, taking another sip of my drink. "Phone's glued to my hand, inbox never empties. We're behind schedule on one site, over budget on another. Just trying to keep the walls from caving in, literally and figuratively."

Link rubbed his head. "Damn, bruh. That bad?"

"Some days, it feels like I'm the only one giving a damn."

"We need to check in with you more," Kenny said. "You've been carrying a lot."

Marcus leaned over and clapped me on the back. "That center means something to you, and we get that. But don't run yourself into the ground trying to build it."

I didn't respond right away. I just rolled the whiskey around in my glass, nodding my head in appreciation.

"I got it," I said, almost too quickly. Then I added, "But yeah... it's been a lot."

"So," Kenny said, exhaling a cloud of smoke. "Music festival's coming up. We rolling through?"

"I might stop by," I said. "Heard they're supposed to have some pretty good bands this year."

Kenny threw up his hands. "Come on, man. Cam's about to be off at camp, and you've been working yourself into the ground. Get your ass outside."

I didn't argue. Most days at work were touch and go—tense, unpredictable, and draining. I'd have to see how I felt when the time came.

* * *

The next morning, my preteen, Cameron, stood with his arms folded beside the open trunk, his duffel bag lying at his feet. The camp drop-off lot was packed. Parents were clinging to their children like they'd never see them again. Counselors who looked no older than college students steered the kids toward check-in tables. The tweens all looked aloof and indifferent, attempting to hide their nervous energy. Cameron wasn't saying much, which said everything.

"You good, bud?" I asked casually, reaching past him to zip up his bag.

He gave me a small shrug, then a tight-lipped nod. "Yeah. It just... got hot out here."

I nodded slowly. "Yup. Summer tends to do that."

He cracked a smirk but didn't meet my eyes.

I bent down to his eye level. "You know you're allowed to be nervous, right? It's your first time at camp and a whole new summer crew. It's a pretty big deal."

"Yeah, but I'm not nervous. I just don't want bunk beds. My friend Justin said last year, in his cabin, he roomed with a kid who kicked the wall all night in his sleep."

"See, this is what journaling is for," I said, pushing his leather-bound notebook into the side pouch. "Write it all down. Horse-kickers, lunch mystery meat, camp crushes. All of it."

He rolled his eyes, but a chuckle escaped. "You're so weird, bro."

I lifted a brow at the "bro" comment, choosing to let it slide... this time. "And yet, incredibly wise. You'll appreciate my weirdness one day."

He pretended to think about it. "Maybe. But... probably not."

I rested a hand on his shoulder. "Cam, I want you to talk to your counselors if you need anything. And if you don't want to talk, just write it out, rip it up, and throw it away. Got that?"

He nodded again. "Got it, Dad."

I pulled him into a quick hug, and to my surprise, he didn't stiffen. In fact, he held onto me a moment longer than usual. When he stepped back, his round eyes held an even mix of bravery and hesitation. Willow's eyes.

"Want me to walk you inside?" I asked, half-longing for an invitation.

"Nah," he said, picking up his bag and slinging it over his shoulder. "I've got it from here."

I gave the top of his head a gentle rub. "Go get 'em, bud."

"Of course, I stay ready." Smirking, he headed toward the registration table. Halfway there, he turned back. "And, Pops, don't get caught crying in the car."

I laughed, caught off guard. "No promises, son."

He grinned, then disappeared into the throng of bodies preoccupied with phones while shuffling toward the main pavilion, sporting the tween uniform of headphones and Crocs.

* * *

Surprisingly, I didn't end up crying. Not right away, at least.

I drove home in pensive silence. No music, no podcasts, not even my normal check-in call with Mom. Wrapped up in the quiet hum of my thoughts, I attempted to sort out how I was feeling about dropping my only child off for sleepaway camp for the next several weeks.

The house was eerily quiet when I walked back in. Cameron's LeBron tennis shoes were parked right by the door. There was a half-eaten bowl of cereal sitting on the edge of the sink, and his CK One cologne faintly lingered in the air. I shook my head. The kid had a gift for leaving traces of himself throughout the house like confetti.

I removed my shoes and hooked my keys on the rack before heading upstairs, taking them two at a time. I plopped down on the edge of my bed before reaching into my wallet and pulling out the photo I always kept tucked directly behind my driver's license. Cameron was standing on the pier in Port Clinton last summer, grinning from ear to ear. He held a white bass in one hand, a framed photo of Willow in the other. That had been his idea. "So Mom can be in the memory, too," he'd said.

I didn't share with anyone how much I still sought her advice. How many decisions I'd made based on what she *would've* said, not what I *wanted.* But as I ran my thumb along the edge of the picture, I asked WWWD, my acronym for What Would Willow Do? She would've packed him extra sunscreen. She would've insisted on calling the camp nurse directly with clear instructions for administering his meds. She would've known just the right words to help him feel more confident. Hell, she would've known what was going on with him years before I stopped making excuses.

Willow wanted to get Cameron tested for ADHD when he was five. I told her he was just "being a boy." That he'd grow out of it. That his teachers didn't understand him like we did. Turned out I was wrong. By the time I came around to the idea, we'd already lost time. Precious time she never got back with him. Time he would never have with her again.

Now, every win—whether it's with parenting, work, or healing—felt like a balancing act instead of being accompanied by joy or ease. Every life choice, school meeting, and doctor's appointment felt delicate, hard-won, like I was holding it all together with a hope and a prayer. I kept showing up for Cameron, for myself. But I was never sure if I was doing any of it right.

I was incredibly lonely. But the idea of experiencing love without her still felt like betrayal. Happiness felt too expensive. Moving forward felt like leaving her behind. Like abandoning a chapter we hadn't gotten to finish writing.

I closed my eyes and fell back on the bed, clutching the photo. I never knew what the hell I was doing. I never felt like I had it. Like I was standing on sturdy ground. But, for

Cameron's sake, I knew I still needed to try. To show up for him like only I could, because the truth was, I was all he had.

Maybe going to the cigar bar with the fellas wasn't about escaping. Maybe it was about remembering the pieces of myself that hadn't disappeared when Willow did. Starting again, even if it felt foreign. Like I wasn't quite ready. Would I ever be?

I opened my eyes and whispered into the stillness of the room.

"I'm trying my best, Low. For Cameron. For you. I always will."

Chapter 3
Tawni

My classroom was finally free of the sounds of tapping pencils, humming smartboards, and cackling third graders who were supposed to be concentrating on their work. The sole ticking of the wall clock and the drone of the air conditioning were soothing after the chaos I'd endured that morning.

Kicking off my sandals and letting my toes stretch beneath my desk, I focused on the past two weeks of summer enrichment. Outside the window, sunlight spilled across the playground in long, golden columns. A couple of kids rode past on bikes, laughing loud and free. A twinge of jealousy caught me off guard.

This was supposed to be my summer, my inner voice reminded me. *The one where I finally focused on myself, my goals, and my new path.*

Instead, I was still here, teaching lessons I barely had the energy to plan. I dug my hand into my messenger bag, brushing past a crushed granola bar and a stack of ungraded journals. I finally pulled out my phone. The home screen was filled with a dozen notifications—none of which I planned to acknowledge at that moment. I pulled up my notes app and looked at the summer goals I'd created a few short months ago: pool days, writing music, maybe a solo trip somewhere warm. I'd even bookmarked a few flights.

But I'd abandoned them for the sake of saying yes to everything except myself. *Cedric owes me big time.* Just as I was about to toss my phone back in my bag, it lit up again.

Dukes Calling.

Sighing, I answered. "Hey, Mom."

Her voice always cut through my darkness like only sunlight can. "Oh, you sound tired, baby."

"Nah, I'm good," I lied automatically. "Just finishing up after a long day."

There was a pause. Then her knowing chuckle sent goosebumps over my skin. "Mmm-hmm. I've been hearing that tired 'ol 'I'm fine' since you started masking your emotions at nine years old—the same age as those students of yours. It still doesn't fool me."

I closed my eyes. It was time to cut the shit. "I love working with my kids, Mom. I really do."

"But...?"

I glanced out the window again. "It's been a year since Dante and I broke up. And this was supposed to be my bounce-back summer."

"Oh, don't I know it. You've been planning this hot girl summer for months. Good books, hot dates, long naps, and grilled shrimp tacos."

I laughed out loud. "And I thought you were tuning me out."

"Never."

After a beat, Mom asked, "So what happened?"

I pressed the phone to my cheek, thinking. "I just... keep

saying yes, Mom. To teaching summer school. To helping the new teachers with their curriculum planning. Even to being on the planning committee for the glow-and-go sendoff party for the last day of summer school."

"Tawni," she said gently. "Why do you think it's so hard to choose yourself?"

I blinked fast, refusing to let my tears fall while at work. "I... I keep thinking if I stay useful and needed, it'll distract me from the feeling that something's missing."

After thinking for a few moments on either end of the line, in a softer voice, Mom said, "Baby, you can be needed *and* be whole. You're not just here to pour into others. You deserve your own moment to shine."

"You're absolutely right," I said, nodding. I really needed that reminder.

We talked a little more, switching to lighter topics. She told me about a new recipe she was trying for dinner, then gave me an unsolicited update on the latest drama with her neighbor's new boyfriend. I smiled through it all, letting her humor distract me for a moment.

When we hung up, I sat and stared at the sunlight stretching across the classroom floor. I pulled out an untouched notebook from my bag where I'd once written some of my best songs. Flipping through the pages and refamiliarizing myself with the words felt foreign. I realized that I really *missed* me.

It was time to do something about that.

* * *

Fresh-cut grass and sunscreen floated in on the morning breeze as I shifted behind the registration table, smoothing my camp volunteer shirt. A volunteer was nervously organizing the glossy pamphlets, flyers, and color-coded cabin rosters as they fluttered around on the table. I tucked a loose curl behind my ear and squinted into the crowd of parents and kids buzzing through the parking lot of the community rec center.

I hadn't planned on doing much this summer—especially not taking on a part-time teaching assignment. But when the volunteer coordinator at Rising Arrow Enrichment Camp called requesting extra hands for camp check-in, I was actually excited to accept. Summer camp had changed so many of my former students' lives. Being here, even just for a few hours, was a great way to still be part of that magic and see some of my old students without a huge time commitment.

"Hey, Ms. Alexander!"

I waved and accepted warm hugs from several familiar faces. They looked a lot taller and more grown-up than they had just a few short years ago, but those bright, hopeful eyes hadn't changed.

"Next in line!" I called cheerfully.

I paused as a figure in the parking lot caught my eye.

A tall, broad-shouldered man was standing just beyond a shaded tent, wearing shades. He didn't move to join the crowd, just shifted his weight from one foot to the other, absently twirling his key ring on his finger. Almost like he wasn't sure if he should stay or go.

The tilt of his head and tension in his frame tugged at my memory.

A few moments later, he abruptly turned on his heel and disappeared into the growing crowd.

I blinked, sorting through my thoughts. The mixture of recognition and disappointment nagged at me. But I didn't have time to dwell. A boy was approaching my table.

"Hi there," I said absentmindedly. My eyes were still on the parking lot. "Can I get your name?"

The boy shuffled closer, toting a duffle bag nearly bigger than he was. He smiled and mumbled, "Hey, Ms. Alexander."

I froze.

Cameron?

My eyes darted down the roster, scanning until I found him: *Edwards, Cameron—Cabin 3, Bunk 12.*

I looked up slowly, and sure enough—there was that familiar mischievous smirk barely hiding behind his excitement. He was taller now, lankier. His neat fade was now carefully styled twists that nearly reached his collarbone. But I would have recognized him anywhere.

"Mr. Cameron Edwards," I teased, smiling wide. "I almost didn't recognize you! You've got some serious height now."

He gave a shy shrug and stuffed his hands into the pockets of his basketball shorts. "Yeah. Puberty or whatever."

Bone-dry humor. Classic Cam.

I laughed and handed him his welcome packet. "Are you excited for your first year of camp?"

He gave a lopsided grin. "I mean... excited for a break from my dad breathing down my neck about keeping my room clean for a few weeks."

I leaned in slightly, lowering my voice. "Those are critical life skills. You'll thank him in about ten years when you get your bachelor pad."

Cameron glanced away, kicking a loose rock. "Yeah, I know. So, how is it here? New places can be... weird."

"I get it," I said softly. "But I think you'll like it. Just keep in mind, first days are weird for everyone. Even adults."

He lifted his eyes to meet mine, revealing the vulnerability hiding beneath his aloof exterior.

"Tell you what," I said, standing and rounding the table to meet him. "How about I walk you to your cabin? We'll scope it out together."

Relief washed over his face. "Ms. Alexander, you don't have to—"

"Cam, I want to," I said, meeting his eyes.

He nodded.

We weaved through the clusters of laughing kids and departing parents. A faint, pleasant smell of fresh-cut wood and campfire smoke lingered in the air. Along the way, I introduced him to a couple of campers who were tossing a football nearby. By the time we reached Cabin 3, Cameron was chuckling at one of the boys' impressions of a camp counselor.

"You'll have a great time," I said, squeezing his shoulder gently.

He smirked. "As long as they're not serving us jail food."

I laughed. "I hear the chicken tenders are decent at best. S'mores are chef's kiss, though."

His smile lit up his whole face, and it calmed my own nerves to see his anxiety begin to subside.

"Here we are," I said, walking him up the steps and pushing open the screen door.

Inside, the cabin was simple but homey. Rows of wooden bunk beds lined the knotty pine walls, each one topped with a neatly folded blanket and a name tag hanging from the bed frame. The floorboards creaked beneath our feet, and the late morning sunlight spilled through the screened windows.

Near the back of the room, a boy around Cameron's age sat on the bottom bunk, carefully unpacking a stack of graphic tees and organizing them in the small cubbies built into the side of the bed. Small, neat braids hung along his face. When he noticed us, he stood and waved.

"Hey, looks like your roommate's already here," I said, smiling.

Cameron tossed his duffel bag onto the top bunk and waved back. "Hey, I'm Cameron."

The boy's face brightened. "Brent. You play Fortnite?"

Cameron's whole demeanor relaxed. "Every single chance I get."

Brent grinned, gesturing toward the dark blue Fortnite hoodie tied around his waist. "Me too. You build or just rush?"

Cameron shrugged. "Depends. Mostly rush. I'm not patient enough to build."

Brent gave a hearty laugh, exposing all of his teeth. "Same, man! I'm all about that action."

I watched as the two boys started animatedly comparing strategies, favorite skins, and weapons. I couldn't feel more grateful. Cam had been through a lot in the past few years, and he deserved to let his hair down and just be a kid for the next few weeks.

Cameron, Brent, and I walked back out to the main court-yard so they could grab snacks and get ready for orientation. Once they were settled in, I waved goodbye, leaving them in the middle of a growing circle of campers who shared a love for online gaming.

It looked like Cam had found his tribe. He was exactly where he needed to be.

An hour later, my shift was over. I packed up to leave, a gentle breeze ruffling my long denim skirt as it slightly cooled the swelling humidity. As I strolled back to my car, I scanned the parking lot, still holding on to the image of that tall, familiar figure in the distance. Although he was long gone, the warmth of Rudolph Edwards' memory stayed with me. It was a pleasant surprise to see Cameron today, but I definitely hadn't expected the complex emotions his father's brief appearance had stirred up in me.

Chapter 4
Rudolph

The music was already spilling out into the street as I pulled into the gravel lot across from Edgewater Park. Steady basslines thumped through my tires like a second heartbeat, loud enough to rattle the rearview mirror. I sat parked and chilled for a moment, letting the car idle. The festival crowd was thick, pulsing with energy. A summer Saturday afternoon I used to live for. Carefree, easy, and wide open with possibilities.

And yet, I didn't move.

Cameron had just completed his first week at Rising Arrow Enrichment Camp, and the silence in the house had been much louder than I'd expected. I wasn't in a sentimental, look-ing-at-his-baby-pictures type of mood, but it had definitely been an I-don't-know-what-to-do-with-myself type of week. For the first time in years, I didn't have to mold my weekend around football practices, multiple trips to the grocery store, or navi-gating his vampire summer sleeping schedule when I had to get up at the crack of dawn for work. I'd planned to use the down-time to get caught up on rest. Hit the gym. Finally clean out the garage. Instead, I spent most evenings refreshing the camp's live feed, hoping to catch a glimpse of Cameron camping or playing glow-in-the-dark laser tag. I'd only spotted him once—photobombing someone else's photo, hood halfway up. He looked like he was having fun. Had a little crew already, and they were rockin' it out. About four of them. Still, I wanted to call up there and check in.

"Give him space," Willow used to say. "Believe me, Cam will bloom when he's ready." Of course, she was right. She always was.

I rubbed the back of my neck. Hanging at the sports lounge last night with the fellas had helped, but only for a minute. They'd gotten me to promise I'd roll through the festival with them tonight. But Marcus had texted the group a couple of hours ago that he was bailing on us for a woman he'd just met while in line to get his license renewed. Link dropped out next —said he tweaked his back trying to relive his glory days in a pickup basketball game with some twenty-somethings who still had full use of their knees. And Kenny never actually says he's not coming. My dude just suddenly fades to black, like he went into witness protection. So as a free man with ample time on my hands, I had no one to spend it with. At least not anyone who would answer my call on the first ring.

I cut the ignition and stepped out into the heat, pressing down hard and drawing sweat from my brow the minute I joined the crowd. I was instantly surrounded by music, laughter, and the aroma of grilled meats. The atmosphere was potent, vibrant, and electric. I slowly wove through the crowd, soaking in the sights. Screeching kids were running wild, toting half-melted popsicles, aunties were line dancing and whipping fans, and the old heads were perched in folding chairs behind tables of incense and shea butter. Cleveland never failed to come alive in the summer. I missed experiencing this in my city.

Grief had a funny way of warping time. It felt like I'd been split in two. Some days I woke up feeling just like my old self again, cracking jokes and planning impromptu weekend trips. Other days, I bore the heaviness of that man standing bedside, clutching Willow's hand and whispering in her ear not to let go. It was like those two sides of me couldn't possibly inhabit the same body and soul. I couldn't even tell the two apart anymore.

Still, I had made it here. I showed up. That was a solid first step. I'd just started scanning the sea of food trucks when the smell of crema-slathered Mexican corn hit me, reminding me I'd skipped lunch. I smiled. Probably for the first time all day. *There you go. Start small. Corn first. Soul-searching later.*

I started heading in that direction and stopped dead in my tracks. There she was. Standing between two food trucks, squinting at a menu while licking sauce off her thumb.

Ms. Alexander, Cameron's third-grade teacher.

Chapter 5
Tawni

I almost didn't come. After a grueling school year, I was excited to focus on myself this summer. To put an end to running on fumes and pushing myself far past capacity. Traveling with my girls. Making bad choices and blaming them all on our youth.

But life stepped in really quick. Since I was covering summer school for Cedric, I'd spent the second week of my summer vacation buried in lesson plans and behavior charts. Another summer detour. Another dream on pause.

Then, to top it off, everyone kept forwarding me Dante's IG posts with his shiny new fiancée. The last one had a caption about "holding out for what's truly yours." Tiff and Trish flooded our group chat with screenshots and angry NeNe Leakes eye roll GIFs, ready to set it off on that fool like Jada. Little did they know I'd just cut all ties with him a couple of weeks ago and had already turned the page.

I found a shaded table where I could soak in the scene while waiting for my girls to arrive. Taking a final bite of my fresh-cut fries, I exhaled in delight. I watched families singing and dancing, lovers cuddling on blankets, and vendors laughing and talking over the music. Okay, this was a cute little vibe and exactly what I needed.

Wiping my hand on a napkin, I checked my vibrating phone. Tiff and Trish were running late. A wardrobe malfunction and a detour later, they'd allowed me to beat them here when I lived almost forty minutes away.

Those fries had done *nothing* to address my raging appetite. I'd skipped lunch that day to save all of my calories for an evening of bad festival food and frozen cocktails. I was looking at the menu, heavily contemplating a Polish boy... or perhaps a pulled pork sandwich when I caught a glimpse of someone standing near the food trucks. I did a double take before I realized who it was. He was really standing right in front of me again.

Rue Edwards.

The first thing I noticed was his height—how he was taller than I remembered. It was my first time seeing him up close and personal in years, but he had that same steadying energy from our virtual parent-teacher meetings. His umber complexion coated his athletic frame, deep, and smooth. I noticed the new lines that had sprouted near his eyes and instantly wondered about the weight he may have been carrying these days. My feet were rooted, and I was unsure whether I should wave or just keep it moving. It had been almost years. I was sure he wouldn't remember me.

But then he looked up—and our eyes locked. His eyes shimmered, and his eyebrows lifted in surprise as recognition quickly set in. He licked those lips, and I was trapped for a moment, trying to stave off the desire rising inside me.

"Miss Alexander?" he said, walking over.

"Mr. Edwards," I said, returning his warm smile. "Wow. It's nice to see you."

He nodded. "Same. I almost didn't recognize you without a bookshelf and a whiteboard behind you."

We laughed, and the tension melted instantly.

"How's Cameron?" I asked.

"Thriving," he said, pride beaming through his eyes. "Just dropped him off at camp. School and sports have been keeping us both on our toes, but he's doing well."

"I love that for him. Middle school's no joke, but it's nothing he can't handle."

He nodded. "Yeah. He's been adjusting pretty well."

"I knew he would. He's bright. Just needed a little support. Tell him I'm proud of him."

"I will. And thanks," he said. "Really. You made a huge difference back then. For both of us."

Heat stained my cheeks. "I receive that. Thanks, Mr. Edwards."

"Please," he said, his voice lowering an octave as he held my eyes for a moment. "Call me Rue."

I nodded, ignoring my thundering pulse in my ears. "Only if you call me Tawni."

Across the plaza, I saw Tiff and Trish approaching, each wearing jean shorts and tanks. They spotted me immediately—and then they laid eyes on him.

Trish pulled Tiff back by the elbow, nodding toward me and Rue.

Even from a distance, Tiff's smirk was clear as day. They stood there sipping their wine slushies, not moving a muscle, as if they were afraid that the slightest movement would interrupt us.

Chapter 6
Tawni

Rue and I chatted for a few minutes before I headed over to greet my friends. With a final wave, I slipped back into the crowd. I glanced over my shoulder and saw him rooted there, in the center of the walkway, watching me walk away.

Imagine my surprise running into Rudolph "Fine Ass" Edwards twice in a week after not seeing him in almost four years. He looked healthy, toned, and scrumptious as hell. It did my heart good to lay eyes on him in person after solely interacting through a screen. Although Rue looked even better than he had a few years ago, I sensed that something was slightly off with him. I'd honed top-notch body language interpretation skills after nearly ten years of teaching, and although he'd flashed a million-dollar smile, the worry lines etched near his eyes told a different story. He was stressed about something. Was it parenting a tween son as a single dad? Whatever it was, it seemed to have Rue tense and exhausted, and it hurt me to see him that way.

Since our brief chat by the food trucks, his presence

lingered like expensive cologne in the atmosphere. I couldn't get his handsome smile off my mind. Over the past hour, I'd spotted him several times in the crowd. Each time we crossed paths and briefly locked eyes, it felt more intense than the last.

Later, I caught him in the crowd again, his head bobbing to the beat of my favorite local reggae band. Then I heard the karaoke host call for volunteers, and before I knew it, I was onstage singing Lauryn Hill with Tiff and Trish like we were at a small dive bar instead of in front of a crowd of hundreds.

Afterwards, Rue strolled up with a proud grin on his face. "Tawni, I had no idea we had the next Lauryn Hill right here in tha Land."

"I could never replace Lauryn. But, yes, I guess I'm multi-talented. Gotta keep folks guessing," I chuckled.

"Well, I'm in awe of you. We need to celebrate. Funnel cake? They smother them in powdered sugar, fresh berries, and fruit puree and top them with whipped cream cheese."

I paused, unsure if this was just dessert or something more. Were we just grabbing a treat together as a kind gesture? Or was there something lingering behind that hopeful glint in his eyes?

Don't overthink it. It's dessert. With a fine-ass man.

"Cream cheese? Now you're speaking my love language. Let's do it," I said.

We grabbed our food and a couple of glasses of wine before finding a nearby table. Savoring each bite, we vibed to the karaoke during intermission. To both of our surprise, a middle-aged white guy sang the hell out of a Bob Marley cut. We cheered him on, holding up our glasses.

"It's been a while since I've been to a festival like this," Rue said, sipping his wine. "Wow, this is really good. What's it called again?"

"Cleveland's own blackberry merlot," I said, taking another sip. "So, why don't you make it to festivals often?"

He shrugged. "Work's been pretty hectic lately. Guess I stopped making time for things like this."

"You're in construction, right?" I asked.

He nodded. "Yeah. Summer's our busiest season, and we have several tight city project deadlines."

I nodded. "Cameron's first year in middle school must have kept you pretty busy too. All of the extra homework and complicated school projects."

"Absolutely. He adjusted pretty well, though. Surprisingly, he's also been helping out around the house more without being asked. I'm still waiting for the other shoe to drop. Like, is this little dude going to invoice me or something?"

"Probably. Knowing Cam, it'll be fully itemized with 'payment due upon receipt' or 'past due' stamped at the top."

We both laughed.

"How about you? How are things at the elementary school?"

"Great. I'm covering for a friend who teaches summer school, which has been a little more than I bargained for," I admitted. "There's always so much to do, and it feels like there's never enough time. But seeing the kids' progress makes it all worth it."

Rue nodded. "Same. Seeing Cameron happy and thriving sustains me through all the practices, meets, and hangouts. Balancing everything isn't easy, though."

"I bet," I said, taking another bite of funnel cake. "This is nice. I forgot what it feels like to just... be outside. With no agenda, no expectations."

"Same here. Lately, my idea of fun is staying awake long enough to watch an entire Netflix episode."

I laughed, reaching out to playfully dap him up.

It felt like I could talk to Rue about everything and nothing. The synergy was easy, light, and fun. The evening sun set and lanterns lit up the festival grounds, and I realized that this was the first time I'd allowed a connection like this since Dante and I broke up. Rue reminded me what it felt like to be fully immersed in getting to know someone. I knew I should thank him for the funnel cake and head back to find my friends. But I couldn't stop smiling. Rue had me feeling like my bounce-back summer wasn't ruined after all. This was an excellent start.

Chapter 7
Rudolph

With every moment that passed, Tawni seemed to grow more comfortable. The more she opened up, the more intrigued I became. The pulsing music and swirling crowds surrounding us faded away as our conversation deepened. We began sharing our struggles and recent challenges with each other, unafraid of how our truths would be received.

"You know, I never thought I'd be a single dad," I confessed. "But here I am, trying to navigate this whole parenting thing on my own. It's true what they say about there being no manual for this shit." I grimaced. The potent wine was loosening my lips. "My bad. Didn't mean to cuss."

"That makes sense," Tawni said, leaning back in her chair. "You've got a lot on your plate—but from the outside looking in, you're making it look easy."

Her smile was soft. "Cameron's lucky."

Her words were simple but exactly what I needed to hear. No judgment. Just compassion and support. "Thanks," I murmured, suddenly overcome with emotion. It took me off guard, but it had been a while since I'd been heard and understood by a woman. "I didn't expect to run into you tonight, but I'm glad I did."

A smile eased across her pretty face. "I need to do better when it comes to carving out time for myself, and today has shown me that there's a need for it."

I nodded. "All you can do is take it one day at a time."

She nodded, taking another bite and licking powdered sugar from those pillowy lips. "You mentioned the challenge of making space for balance as a busy dad with a demanding career. Any plans to change that?"

I leaned back in the chair and rubbed my face, recognizing that Tawni was used to focusing on others and shied away from the spotlight. I'd like to change that. "That's an area of my life that needs improvement. Cam's needs often trump mine due to his need for a solid schedule. My older sister offers to help with him, but I try not to ask her for anything. Her kids are grown, and I want her to enjoy this second act of her life."

Nodding, Tawni said, "That's understandable. But, also, hey pot, I'm kettle."

When she gave a little wave with a tight-lipped grin, I almost lost it. "Touché."

"Just saying. What's your work schedule like?"

"It was out of hand until just recently. I put strong boundaries in place, and although it will create more stress for me to try to fit a 60-hour workload into a 40-hour schedule, I'll be in by seven and off by four every day starting next week. I rarely need to travel, so I can still make it to all of Cam's after-school and weekend events." I saw her nod, as if mentally noting something. "I like the flexibility my career gives me, and I love the work. So, as long as my company honors my needs, I can easily see myself working as a project manager until retirement."

"That's great. I'm happy you've found that balance. That's a lot more than most of us. Most of my friends—myself included—are still figuring that out."

Suddenly, Tawni let out a squeal, and for a moment, my fight or flight mode kicked in.

"Sorry, but my favorite reggae band is performing. They're local, and I've been following them for years," she said, her eyes lighting up. She began moving her hips in the seat, closing her eyes and humming along with the mellow melody. My heart danced right along with her as I watched her for a few long moments before glancing away. The next thing I knew, she was on her feet and pulling me out of my chair.

"Dance with me, Rue Edwards." Her piercing eyes were fixed on me. There was no sign of trepidation on her face. This was a woman who knew what she wanted. So who was I to deny her this moment?

As soon as I was on my feet, she led the way into the crowd, and we eased toward the stage to share a dance. We swayed in time to the music, respecting each other's space. But by the third song, the full effect of the wine had kicked in. Our bodies moved in sync with the thrumming bass line and the sensual melody of the music. As the singer serenaded us, our movements followed paths of their own. Tawni turned her back to me and placed my hands on her hips, which were undulating to the beat. She reached up and encircled the back of my neck, pulling me closer to her. She wound her body, and I matched her tempo, focusing on the feel of her pressed against me. I tried not to overthink where to put my hands or my breathing. This was uncharted territory, and I didn't want to mess up a single second of it.

Emotions ran high, and we lost ourselves in each other, the barriers between us crumbling away with each delicious moment. Under the flickering stage lights, my eyes devoured her, sweeping from her toned thighs peeking from below her white tennis skirt up to the waist beads sinking into her luminous skin. Although desire coursed through me, I resisted a primal urge to be even closer to her, to feel her body tightly pressed against mine without the hindrance of clothes.

The final song reached its climax, and Tawni turned to face me with an intense gaze that said everything she couldn't. She pressed her body against mine, and I felt her quickening heartbeat racing through her chest. In that fleeting moment, I felt an irrevocable shift between us. The spark of attraction ignited into a boisterous flame that threatened to consume us both. Her lips parted, and before she could take her next breath, I leaned down and kissed her.

Her kiss tasted like blackberry and plum, rich and sweet from the wine. We continued exploring each other while preserving the sensual sway of our dance. Her wandering hands spanned the width of my chest, easing up to my neck before cascading down my arms. I kept my hands planted on her hips, afraid of what moving them might very well incite on the makeshift dance floor among thousands of festival-goers.

Just before the song ended, she pulled back, stiffened, and stood stock still. Her eyes were fixed on something in the distance, as if she were a deer caught in headlights. Then a crack of thunder, followed by a sudden downpour of rain, sent the crowd scattering in various directions. It took us a few moments to break our embrace, and once we did, we gazed at each other, each attempting to understand the magnitude of our decision to give in to our desires. The warm rain fell in sheets, soaking our clothes. Tawni took my hand, and we began to sprint, seeking shelter beneath a nearby tent.

The folding chairs had been removed, so we sat on the abandoned six-foot vendor table. Chests heaving, we fought to catch our breath. Women attempted to salvage their fresh hairstyles and designer outfits while making a mad dash toward the parking lot. A lady in a sundress with a long train kicked off her stilettos, scooped them up, and ran after a man who was sprinting at least ten feet ahead of her.

"Shady as hell," we said in unison, then laughed.

After a pregnant pause, Tawni turned to me and said, "Look, Rue. About what just happened out there, I know I initiated things," she paused, licking her lips. "I want to know your thoughts on it."

I blinked, puzzled by her serious expression. "My thoughts? It was exhilarating."

She nodded, her eyes still searching mine. "For me, too. I just needed a little clarity before we went any further. Have you been dating?"

Searching her eyes, I picked up a hint of concern. "If I'm being honest, not regularly. I haven't even introduced anyone new to Cam. But spending time with you tonight has been nice. I'm open to exploring something with you."

She nodded. "I've had a great time with you tonight, Rue. And it's great that you're open to dating. But it's one thing to share a dance and a kiss at a music festival and a whole other thing to begin dating one another. I don't want to put my desires before Cameron's needs. It sounds like he's adjusting well to his new school and making friends. He's doing so well right now... I'd hate to shake that up."

The concern in Tawni's eyes affirmed what I already knew about her. She carried a deep sense of responsibility for the people around her and carefully weighed how her actions might affect others. It was an admirable quality, which made me want her even more. "I get it. But honestly, Cameron adores you. It wouldn't be a disruption—it'd be a bonus." I chuckled before sharing, "When he found out I was coming here tonight, he challenged me to come home with at least three 'hot chick's digits.' I think it's safe to say he's ready for me to get back out there."

We shared a quick laugh.

I reached for her hand. "I've been letting fear lead me for the past few years. But tonight... with you... this doesn't feel scary."

Tawni offered a small, thoughtful smile, but I could still see the hesitation in her eyes. I couldn't do anything but respect that because I felt it too.

"Okay, we don't have to rush anything," she said gently. "Let's just take our time. See where this goes."

The rain was still falling in a soft mist, but neither of us made a move to leave the tent. We sat there for a while, side by side on the table, as the festival slowly wound down around us.

We agreed to talk more soon. Maybe grab a bite, catch a show, something light and easy.

"Next weekend?" I asked.

Tawni tapped her chin dramatically, pretending to think.

Giving her side-eye, I said, "I'll take that as a yes."

She bumped her shoulder into mine and I fought back an excited grin. We stood and stepped out into the night. I began walking her to her car.

"I spotted my friends earlier," she said, scanning the near-empty parking lot.

"The two ladies you performed with on stage? My bad, I didn't mean to interrupt girls' night," I said.

"No, they were doing their own thing. But I know they aren't going to leave me here alone."

"Say less. They don't know anything about me, nor do they trust me. I have a sister, so I know all about girl code," I chuckled.

"Yeah, they don't play," she said, disarming her car alarm.

We both looked up to see her friends standing a few rows

over under an umbrella, watching us like hawks. I gave them a wave, and they waved back, sizing me up like they were memorizing every last detail about me.

"Well, Tawni, this has been an incredible evening. Thanks for sharing it with me," I said, opening her door for her.

She looked up at me with those big round eyes, and I had to fight the urge to lean down, take her face in my hands, and kiss her again.

"I enjoyed myself and I'm looking forward to hearing from you. As a matter of fact," she said, handing me her phone with her contacts screen open. "I'm not about to play the waiting game with fate. Put your number in."

I took it, smiling. "I was just about to ask you to do the same."

After I typed in my number, I handed her mine. She took a selfie of us right there on the sidewalk—her damp hair curling from the rain, both of us grinning wide—and set it as my contact photo.

"That way I'll always remember this moment when you text," she said, slipping the phone back into her purse. "No pressure, Rue. But I hope you do."

"Bet on that," I said.

Smiling, she slipped into the car.

"Get home safe," I said, closing the door. "As a matter of fact, text me when you do."

"You got it."

I looked up and saw her friends get into an SUV.

She started her car, looked up, and gave me another smile.

After all these years of thinking about her, she was still the same sweet woman I remembered. I'd already lost time with her once. I wasn't about to let it happen again. I wanted to pursue the possibility of what a relationship with Tawni could look like.

Chapter 8
Tawni

I woke up the next morning hugging my body pillow and smiling. Vivid dreams of dancing with Rue, my body pressed into his, clung to the edges of my mind and I didn't want to open my eyes. I hadn't slept this well in months. Maybe even years.

His name was etched in the back of my mind, glowing with full luminosity. That kiss was electric. Our conversation was captivating. Our dance was chemistry in motion. I turned onto my side, instinctively reaching for my phone, checking for a good morning text. It always sounded corny coming from other guys, but I was looking forward to receiving one from him because I knew it would be genuine.

My eyes widened as I looked at the time. It was barely past eight, and I was already pressed like a Sunday morning paper for more of him. I checked anyway. No new messages. The last one was him telling me goodnight after I let him know I was home.

I sighed, flopping onto my back again and staring at the ceiling. I was *not* about to overthink this shit. I would let our beautiful night be just that—beautiful. No promises of happily ever afters. It just was what it was.

Then my phone buzzed. Twice. The Triple Threat text group.

Trish: Okay, we've given you your space. Time's up.

Tiff: Brunch at our spot. 11. Be ready to bring the stories and don't be a moment late, bitch.

Of course.

Reluctantly, I stretched and threw my legs over the edge of my bed. After nearly a year of nothing but a bunch of failed first dates, it was time to be lovingly ravaged by my besties for every last detail of my time with Rue.

I was the first to arrive at our favorite little café, already sipping my iced lavender latte on the outdoor patio. Summertime brunch was always a fashion show for our little crew. We took every opportunity to look our finest during the narrow margin of warm weather in Cleveland.

My wide-brimmed straw hat was tilted low over oversized sunglasses and a cropped tee knotted at the waist. My lime green skirt with a thigh-high slit offered optimum flair and function. Sandals laced delicately around my ankles, completing my soft girl era look.

Tiff strolled up in ripped light-wash jeans that hugged her curves, a crisp off-the-shoulder white blouse, and clear studded heels. A gold chain rested on her collarbone like punctuation. She didn't say a word as she air-kissed me and took a seat—her attitude did all the talking.

Then there was Trish, fashionably late and unapologetic. Her ruched cream skirt, balanced by a vintage-style crop top plastered with colorful graphics, was complemented by layered pearls and amber-tinted shades, serving up old-school glam. Her tiny green handbag made a wordless bold statement. Once Trish took her seat, they both side-eyed me with their arms folded, wearing matching smirks.

"Okay, so spill it all," Tiff said before I could even ask what they thought of the festival. "And don't play in our faces, secret squirrel."

"So, y'all really waited until the morning, huh?" I teased, setting down my drink. "I thought for sure I'd have six voice-mails by the time I got home."

Trish leaned in. "We saw you walk out with him. The way y'all were all hugged up, we figured you were talking to him the whole way home."

"Yeah, we let y'all have your little moment," Tiff said, her eyes sweeping me up and down.

I looked her up and down right back. "Little?"

"Yes, little. You barely know him," Tiff reminded me.

"We just mildly observed y'all here and there. From what we saw, it looked... fiery," Trish said in an island accent, adding a shoulder roll. "So, how was it?"

I laughed, catching her nod to the Caribbean flavor of the evening. I sipped my latte and took a moment to respond. "It was... very nice."

They both groaned.

"Nice?" Trish repeated. "Girl, that man had you floating across that parking lot. You were glowing."

Tiff tooted up her lips. "Right. Don't play in our faces, sis. What's with all the secrecy?"

I shrugged. "Okay, yeah. He's really sweet, and we had a great time talking all night."

"And dancing. And kissing," Trish added with a. Wink.

I lifted a brow. "But you were only 'mildly observing?' Anyway, things felt easy between us. I really enjoyed myself."

Tiff leaned in. "So, who was he? We know you already knew him because y'all seemed kind of familiar with each other. Plus, you've never let a guy get that close to you that quickly."

I sighed dramatically. My girls knew me too well and were keeping close tabs, per usual. "Do y'all remember my student Cameron from a few years back? He lost his mom just before the pandemic hit."

Trish leaned back in her seat. "I do remember you mentioning that. You were working really closely with his father after that to get Cameron an Individualized Education Plan."

Tiff's eyes bulged. "Shut. Up. That was *Thee* Rudolph Edwards who you've been obsessed with for years?"

"Okay, obsessed is a reach, and you know it," I said, pointing my finger at her. "But yes. Rue and I... ran into each other last night."

"*Rue?*" Trish and Tiff exclaimed in unison as we grabbed our plates and stood to browse the brunch buffet. Then they wagged their tongues, cackled, and high-fived each other.

I looked around, embarrassed. "Will y'all pipe down, please?"

Tiff gathered herself, then grabbed a Belgian waffle. "Well the man can move. Had you channeling your inner bad gal RiRi on the dance floor."

"She's a real island gal now," Trish teased before she broke into song. "Work, work, work, work, work, work!"

We laughed. Then Tiff leaned in closer. "Did it feel weird at first, slow grinding on your student's daddy?"

I thought for a moment. "I was super guarded at first. It did feel a little off, but I think it was mostly because I made it feel that way, you know?"

They each nodded as we helped ourselves to the crispy bacon.

"But he was just as genuine as before. The way he talked about parenting, grief, and balancing it all was touching. And he made it a point to ask about me and how I've been."

Tiff's grin softened. "Aww. That's good, Tawn."

"And let the record show," Trish added, pointing a perfectly manicured nail at me, "this only happened because we were late. So, in other words, you're welcome."

Rolling my eyes as we sat back down at our table, I said, "Finally, your rude behavior landed in my favor."

"So now that you're out here in these dating streets again, we expect regular updates. And we're approving your wardrobe choices for the next five dates," Tiff informed me as she dipped her French toast in syrup. "Not that we don't trust you, but these circumstances are dire."

"Oh, it's already on the books, my G," I said, biting into a sausage link. "I'm inviting him to my show tonight."

Trish whooped. "Look at you! Scheduling dates like a grown-ass woman with healed trauma!"

I laughed. "Don't gas me."

"So we'll get to meet Mr. Durty Wine up close and personal tomorrow?" Tiff asked.

"You will," I sang, doing my best to contain my excitement.

"Bet," Tiff said, raising a toast with her pineapple mimosa. "To growth, new beginnings, and finally not being the awkward fifth wheel."

"Cheers to that," I said, clinking my cup to their glasses.

The conversation drifted. We caught up on Trish's latest date fiasco and Tiff's growing novelty candle business. But eventually, they caused the good vibe to shift with their messiness.

"Did you see what Dante posted this morning?" Trish asked, showing me her phone.

I hesitated to take the phone from her but decided to just get it over with. The photo hit me square in the face like a sucker punch. Dante was dressed in all white with an arm draped around his fiancée. It looked like an engagement brunch. They were surrounded by a smiling group of well-wishers holding champagne flutes. I recognized many of the faces in the crowd as his friends and family.

I handed the phone back to her. "Trish, I didn't ask for this. And respectfully, I'm good on the updates."

The girls looked at each other before staring at me in shock.

"Look, I know y'all mean well," I sighed. "But I'm not interested in knowing how his story ends. I'm too busy writing my own to care anymore."

Tiff reached across the table and squeezed my hand. "Got it. His ass is in the rearview, friend."

Trish nodded, placing her hand on top of both of ours. "Right, forget him. It's always been Team Tawni. Always will be."

I met each of their eyes and smiled. "Thanks, lovies. Now, are y'all ready to go shopping? I've got to look good enough to eat tonight."

* * *

On the drive home, I put on a 90s R&B playlist and let my thoughts drift. I thought about the solo date I planned for myself next week—a glassblowing class. Afterward, I would walk around, grab ice cream, sit in the park, and look at the waterfall. I thought about my upcoming gig Friday night at the lounge.

Then I thought about Rue—his warm brown eyes, that easy

laugh. I wanted to rush into this heart-first, all gas, no brakes. But I still heard the loud, clear voice of my ex echoing in my mind.

"You have more issues than Vogue."

"No one wants a woman who needs all this damn reaffirming."

I turned the volume up and drowned him out. That voice didn't hold weight around here anymore.

When I got home, I slipped into my favorite oversized tee and biker shorts before lighting Tiff's strawberry shortcake candle. It looked like a decadent dessert from a bakery display and was almost too pretty to burn. As soon as I lit the wick, the room began to fill with the mouthwatering scents of fresh strawberries, vanilla bean, and buttery shortbread—cozy and inviting.

"My sis is so talented," I murmured, curling up on the couch with a book, determined to reclaim the peace I'd been nurturing all day. Dante would not win.

After about two chapters, my phone buzzed.

Rue: How was your day? Counting down the moments until our date.

My heart thudded in my chest. I typed a response before I could second-guess myself.

Me: Hung with the girls, now I'm chillin' at the house. I have a show at Cherry's Lounge tonight. You should come hang.

Rue: Say less. I'll be the guy in the crowd pretending not to watch your every move.

Me: Pretending? You better be front row, mouthing all the words like a groupie.

Rue: Bet. Send 'em now and I'll make it happen.

I laughed, sharing the notes of my list of cover songs.

Rue: No Sleep Tonight by Mýa? Demon Time by Alex

Vaughn? Moment by Victoria Monét? Exactly what kind of show is this?

Me: Definitely NSFW, lol It's not my usual lineup, but I'm following a poetry lounge. Have to bring the heat to keep the vibe going.

Rue: This is going to be hot, alright. Now I'm really counting down 🔥

I smirked and shook my head, setting my phone down on the armrest and returning to my book. He had no idea what he was in store for. Class was officially dismissed, and he was about to meet Summertime Tawni—legs, vocals primed and ready, and surely not here to play. In a few short hours, I was going to blow this man's mind.

Chapter 9
Tawni

The low hum of the bass pulsed through the walls, but in the back office of Cherry's Lounge, it was just me and my playlist. Holding my compact mirror, I leaned in to add a final swipe of lip gloss to my lips, pressing them together until they glistened. Surprisingly, my twist-out was still voluminous from my bantu knots earlier that week, and my customized oversized bamboo hoops gave my whole Bohemian look its final finish.

Normally, my nerves would've been shot, but after a ten-minute FaceTime with Trish and Tiff, I was ready to own that stage. They were disappointed they couldn't be there in person, but they'd hyped me up so good I could've floated to the mic. That's the thing about them ride-or-dies—when they know how to properly gas you up, it's like nothing else in this world.

"Alright, Ms. Tawni, you ready?" Tip, the barback who doubled as a stage manager, peeked through the cracked door.

I nodded.

"Good, 'cause you're up!"

"Thanks, Tip," I said, taking a deep breath, rolling my shoulders, and tucking my phone into my clutch. Showtime.

As I walked down the narrow hallway, I was greeted by the rich scents of bourbon, citrus, and candle wax. Vision, a well-known local poet, walked up wearing a form-fitting dress and an intricate headwrap. She leaned in for a hug.

"You're going to kill it, Tawni. I'll be singing along in the audience."

"Thanks, sis." I peeked out at the crowd. The house was packed, per usual. Couples sat close, paired up in red leather booths. A few regulars were posted up at the bar, nodding along to the DJ's slow, sensual groove. The stage glowed under soft, amber lights, projecting long shadows over the crowd. But my eyes were only searching for one thing. My eyes couldn't find him. But I felt him. When my vision finally landed on Rue sitting near the back, just left of center, I released a long breath. He hadn't spotted me yet. But he would.

Tonight wasn't just about a setlist or vocals—it was about showing up for myself. Letting Rue see exactly what he'd signed up for was just the cherry on top. I caught the tremor just as I was setting down my glass of water and smoothing the front of my black crop top. I kept my eyes trained on the setup, pretending not to notice the man who'd just made my pulse spike.

The venue had a cozy intimacy to it—low lights, vintage furniture, and walls painted in jewel tones that hugged like a warm embrace. My stage name was printed on the chalkboard by the bar: *Tonight's Feature: T. Lexx, Live at 8 PM.*

I stood in the back, chopping it up with the drummer for a few minutes. I looked up and saw a few friends from work sitting near the front, waving from their plush velvet booth. I smiled and returned their greeting, but my eyes kept flicking to the back of the bar. To the tall, commanding, casual man sitting in a slate button-down with the sleeves pushed up to his elbows, muscular forearms resting on the edge of the table. He was sipping something dark and neat. Our eyes met, and he slowly lifted his drink, a subtle smile tugging at the corners of his mouth.

My stomach flipped. I couldn't remember the last time I'd invited a man to come hear me sing. But he'd come, just like he promised, and I realized what I felt wasn't just nerves; it was anticipation.

"Folks," the emcee called out from center stage, "how're you enjoying yourselves so far?"

He was answered by catcalls, whistles, and applause.

"That's what I like to hear. I hope you enjoyed the poetry; now it's time for some soulful R&B. So give it up for the beautiful, sensational songstress, T. Lexx!"

Applause rang out, and I stepped into the center of the small stage. I kept my expression calm and my shoulders relaxed. But my heart was doing the damn percolator in my chest.

I nodded to the pianist and cued up the first song—an original. Sultry, mid-tempo, full of yearning. It told the story of love neglected and left simmering too long on the back burner. The mic soon grew warm in my hand, and the feathery notes flowed easily, each word soaked in intention. Before long, the audience faded, and it was just me and the music. And Rue.

I felt the full weight of his gaze as I finished the song. I worked the crowd, singing to all sides and got them waving their hands in the air and swaying to the beat. When I started the next one, I felt the shift in the room. This was one of my favorites because of the sultry confidence and quiet power it took to perform it. My ego kicked in, and I sang the entire song as if I were blessing the audience with a once-in-a-lifetime experience.

Rue's head bobbed to the beat, and he mouthed the words along with me.

"Finally, you can add this moment to your memory, oooh," I sang, hitting a high note and tapping my rocking hips in time to the song's sultry rhythm.

I sang to him like he was the only one in the audience. I didn't look away for a moment as I sang the riff. Our eyes locked and the corner of his mouth quirked up, like he knew he'd been caught staring and didn't care. My hips rolled to the sultry beat, and his eyes followed. The guy sitting next to him tried to engage him in conversation, but he was too far gone. I laughed inwardly. Let him watch.

Halfway through the second song, I dipped into something slower, more intimate. I poured every bit of my truth into the lyrics. After my ex's shenanigans that week, I was too tired to pretend. I knew the ache of disappointment almost like the back of my hand, and I was tired of clinging to the empty sweetness of hope. I had to make the song cry.

Glancing over at Rue, I noticed him shift slightly in his seat. His drink sat forgotten. The firm line of his tightened jaw flexed, like he was slowly, painfully coming undone. Most men I dated didn't get access to this part of me. I kept my shows under wraps due to the rawness I exuded on stage. That was a private party—only for me and my audience. But Rue was experiencing my full stage aura on damn near day one, in vivid color. Feeling its full impact and absorbing its intoxicating effect. He wasn't just sitting there listening to me sing. He was intentionally digesting every word, every run, and matching each breath.

When I sang the last notes of "Honey" by John Legend and Muni Long, the room erupted in cheers. I waved, blew kisses, and took my final bow before nodding at the pianist and stepping off the stage. My body vibrated with adrenaline and high energy.

After grabbing my things from the back office, I made my way out to the lounge. I didn't have to scan the crowd to find him. Rue was already moving toward me, watching me intently, like gravity had picked a side.

And spoiler alert—it picked mine.

As he waited for the small crowd of fans to disperse, the poor guy looked like a man caught in a spell, his stride slow but sure. I couldn't help the smile tugging at my lips as I stole glances at him waiting near the bar. Pretending not to notice how his eyes dipped briefly—respectfully, but noticeably—over the curves I'd displayed just for him tonight was difficult.

"You sang like you were trying to incite a riot in here," he said, handing me a generous bouquet of orange dahlias, spray roses, and carnations.

I accepted them and took a slow sniff. "Thanks, these are beautiful. So, did I succeed?"

Rue released a slow breath, then groaned, stopping just short of touching me. "Maybe a few heart palpitations."

"Well, as long as yours is still functioning," I teased, reaching for the glass of water the bartender had set down.

"Barely," he murmured. "You... lit that stage up, T. Lexx."

"And here I thought you came for the rib platter."

He chuckled, relaxing a bit. "Nah, you were definitely the headliner."

I leaned back against the bar, amused at how hard he was working to keep things casual while his whole body betrayed him. "So," I said, sipping slowly. "Was it the vocals or... something else that did you in?"

He didn't miss a beat. "Definitely the whole package. Your stage presence is larger than life."

I smiled shyly. "I see you're generous with the compliments tonight."

"I'm not ashamed to admit your performance had me in a chokehold."

I raised a brow. "A chokehold?"

He nodded solemnly. "One of those dramatic slow-motion, crowd's-cheering-but-I-don't-want-to-tap-out kind of chokeholds."

I cackled. "Sounds pretty intense. You sure you can handle the next one?"

Rue rested one elbow on the bar, angling his body toward mine. "I'll grab one more drink, then I'll tell you exactly how I plan to survive it."

The bartender returned and took his order, then Rue turned his attention back to me.

"Okay, so when's your next show?" he asked, his tone a little more reverent.

"Next Thursday. Different spot. Same energy."

"I'll be there. There's no way I'm missing another second of the T. Lexx experience."

A slow, rising heat thrummed in my chest, and I leaned into it, letting the electricity surge between us like it had every right to be there. Because maybe it did.

Chapter 10
Rudolph

I was in no way prepared for what I experienced that night.

The second Tawni walked onto that stage, something in the atmosphere changed. The casual chatter of the crowd softened, and heads were on swivel. I noticed a sea of phones lifting, as if the crowd knew exactly what was in store.

She didn't walk so much as glide, chin lifted, curls bouncing lightly, framing her jawline. Her outfit was bold—midriff bare, wide-legged pants hugging her curves like they were custom-made for her. But it was her energy. Unbothered, commanding, and deliciously dangerous.

I swear, my pulse spiked on sight. I should've taken a sip of my drink or done something to cool the heat creeping up the back of my neck. But I just... stared. Shit. I was completely captivated. I started getting worried when my chest tightened. I gripped the table, wondering if I was going into cardiac arrest.

Then she opened her mouth and sang. Her voice was smoke and silk—smooth with just enough grit to cut straight through to the core of me. She didn't just hit the notes. She owned every one of them. Rode the beat like she'd broken it in herself. Made every lyric sound like a secret whispered in my ear—graceful, powerful, and made to obey her rhythm.

That was when I realized I'd been clenching my jaw. Forcefully. I shifted in my seat, willing my body to relax, but it was no use. Tawni had me. Every note, every word she sang was a slow, torturous unraveling. Each run and breathy vibrato pulling on a new thread. My bourbon sat untouched and long forgotten, along with my buddy from work. Nothing existed in that moment except her.

Tawni wasn't just exceptionally talented. She strolled out embodying every vivid fantasy I'd quietly suppressed since our first Zoom meeting several years ago, but it wasn't even that. It was the way she commanded attention from the entire room from the moment she walked on stage without having to demand it. The soft light enhanced her skin, and her mouth curved as she serenaded the crowd with confidence and ease. Hell, at one point I was pretty sure she was singing right *through* the crowd... just to reach me. And I must've been right because for a sweet moment, when her eyes caught mine... we were locked in. That invisible string, that unrelenting pull between us, was present all over again. And this time I couldn't blame it on curiosity or coincidence. It was pure *intention*.

I knew, right then and there, this wasn't just an innocent crush. I wasn't just into Tawni Alexander. I wasn't just attracted to her. I was *hooked* on her. She'd mastered a balance of subtle strength and delectable softness that was undoing me.

By the time the track faded and she hit that final note, I wasn't sure who needed a moment of recovery more—her or me. But I knew one thing: if this was the version she felt safe showing me now—God help me—I was starving for the rest.

* * *

It was Sunday, which meant church in the morning and check-ins with the women I'd been dodging all week. Not because I didn't want to see them, but because I'd been too caught up in everything else—work, keeping tabs on Cam, and, if I was being honest, thoughts of Tawni.

The service was solid. Pastor's message hit right where I needed it: grace for yourself and grace for others. We're all doing the best we can with what we have. After the benediction, I lingered longer than I meant to. That's how they get you —the aunties in the congregation, the ones who remember when you were running around with snotty noses and untied laces.

"Rue, how's baby boy doing? Pastor asked us to pray for him during Bible study while he's at camp." Sister James stopped as she passed me, leaning on her bamboo cane. She'd cornered me right next to the exit.

"He's doing well, Sister James. Really enjoying himself."

"Is he still doing that robotics stuff?"

"He is. And science. I'm praying he puts it to good use one day."

She nodded, satisfied. "Keep pouring into that baby. You're doing good by him."

Before I could thank her, my sister appeared at my side, tugging at my elbow like we were still kids.

"Hi Sister James. Always love that purple hat on you," Chandler called as the older woman waved and shuffled away. She turned to me, her eyes tight. "Rue, can I talk to you? But not here," she said under her breath, glancing toward our mother, who was caught up in a conversation across the sanctuary.

65

Without another word, we stepped out into the parking lot.

"So, I have a date tonight," she blurted out. "I met him online. Please don't mention it to Mom. She thinks everything digital is a scam or a direct gateway to murder."

I chuckled. "I won't. But tell me about him."

"He's been pretty cool so far. We've had a few phone conversations and have a lot in common. But you know I haven't dated in forever. Now that I'm an empty nester, I feel like I've forgotten how to do this."

"We're in the same boat here, sis. Look for a man who follows God and has a plan. And don't tell him what you're looking for in a partner up front."

She frowned. "Why not?"

"Because it's nothing for the wrong kind of man to find enough motivation to morph into exactly what you describe."

Chandler lifted a hand. "*Well,*" she riffed in her best choir voice.

After high-fiving her for hitting that high note, I continued. "But the hard part is maintaining that energy. I suggest taking notes and giving him plenty of room to show you exactly who he really is during these first few interactions. If he's faking, he won't be able to do it for long."

She nodded. "Now that you mention it, I noticed as soon as I told him how important it was for my man to be saved, he offered to meet me at church today, but—" she made an exaggerated show of looking around "—where's homeboy at?"

We laughed. My sister and I were pretty reserved, but we brought out the best sides of each other.

"Yeah, that's a red flag, but not necessarily a dealbreaker. Maybe something happened and he got caught up."

"We'll see," she said, shaking her head. "But Rue, you have no idea how much this helps. I knew you were the right person to ask."

"You got it, Channy," I said. "Anytime."

We parted ways, and I headed home after finding Mom and giving her a hug. A couple of hours later, I was kicked back watching the Guardians game when my phone buzzed.

Cam: Yo, Dad. You won't believe what just happened at lunch.

Since Cam only had limited phone access at camp, I called him instead of texting back.

"Yo, you good?" I asked when he answered.

"Yeah," Cam said. It sounded like he was outside. I could hear wind and distant chatter in the background. "But this kid, Rafi, scarfs down six pieces of chili cheese pizza. Next thing we know, he projectile pukes all over the table and his Crocs. It was gross and amazing at the same time."

"Sounds about right for camp," I said, popping a Flamin' Hot Cheeto in my mouth.

He laughed. "But that's not even the craziest part. Right before that, Rafi was being super loud and mean while arguing with another kid—Eli, I think—for no reason. Nobody here really likes that guy."

Baseball game long forgotten, I sat up a little straighter, leaning forward while allowing him to get the full story out.

Cam paused for a moment before continuing. "Rafi even tried to clown me one day last week. Was making fun of how I talk and had something slick to say about my hair. I told him to chill, kinda stepped to him. Gave him the Killmonger mean mug, and he backed right off."

Knowing he was doing it too, I crossed my hands in an X across my chest in solidarity. *Wakanda forever.* "But you're alright?"

"Yeah. I handled it myself. No need to get a counselor involved."

I didn't want to overreact, but I'd recently learned to read between the lines with Cam. He wasn't always forthcoming with his emotions. "I'm proud of you for standing up for yourself, Killa Cam. That took major guts. But... how did you feel about it afterward?"

He was quiet for a second before saying, "I was annoyed at first. Mostly 'cause I'm pretty low-key. I know I tend to talk fast when I'm excited, and sometimes my words blend together."

I nodded, thankful for the years of speech therapy Willow had insisted on.

"But I'm cool now. Brent—my bunkmate—had my back too. He started shouting for Rafi to mind his business, but I let him know I had it. Dude needed to hear it straight from me."

That settled me a little. "You handled that well. If he ever gets out of line, you can always talk to someone. Knowing when to ask for help is important. That doesn't make you weak."

"I know. I promise I will if it gets bad. But now I have major ammo if he tries to come for me again."

"Right. That dude needs to lay low for a minute. But just say the word, and I'll be up there faster than those chili cheese-encrusted Crocs on sports mode."

He howled with laughter; this time it was the high-pitched one I lived for.

I smiled, relishing it for a long moment before adding, "Look, I'm really proud of you, Cam. Sounds like you're doing great out there."

"I am. It's actually fun here," he said, his voice kicking up an octave. "Oh! And I almost beat the top time for finishing laps in my group at swim yesterday."

I sat back again, pride swelling. "Now that's what I like to hear. Keep doing your thing, little man."

"I will. Gotta go. They're calling us for canoeing."

"Stay safe and have fun. I love you, Son."

"Love you too, Dad."

For a few seconds after hanging up, I let my thoughts run their course as I stared at the ceiling. Out of all my life's accomplishments, parenting Cam made me the proudest. It was also one of the hardest things I'd ever done. It was in moments like this that I truly hoped I was doing it all right.

Chapter 11
Rudolph

fter the Guardians added another victory to the books, I glanced at the time. It was almost four. Tawni and I had plans. We were meeting at the park and riding out to Akron together. I wasn't sure if this counted as our second or third date—did the festival and Cherry's Lounge both qualify? Either way, I couldn't lie: this was the one I'd been looking forward to the most.

She pulled up about a minute after I did, looking stunning in a turquoise sundress that knocked my brain offline for a second. After trying my best not to gawk at her, we exchanged a lingering hug. The sparkle in her eyes told me both of us had been thinking about this moment all day.

We were headed to House Three Thirty for R&B Cabaret Night, and the laid-back vibe was exactly what I needed. Throwback soul, delicious foods, and drinks strong enough to make the crowd believe they could successfully hit every one of those Mariah Carey notes.

The ride to Akron was thirty minutes of easy laughter, flowing conversation, and occasional teasing. I liked how natural things felt with Tawni. There were no awkward silences, no scrambling to fill the space, and she was just as curious about me as I was about her.

"So, do you have any siblings?" she asked, shifting in her seat to face me more directly.

"Yup. One older sister. Chandler. She's always acted like my second mama. Swears she knows what's best for me at all times." I chuckled. "She's got a big heart, though. And she's a great aunt to Cameron. I'd do anything for her."

Tawni smiled. "I can relate. I've got a second mama, too. Jaclyn. We're not super close, but we're working on it. It's weird how childhood dynamics never quite go away, even when you're grown."

"Right," I nodded. "You hit thirty but still feel like you're eight when you argue."

We both laughed at that.

"What about hobbies?" I asked. "That's when you're not killin' it on stage or shaping young minds."

"I love being outside—hiking, zip lining, anything with a thrill. Travel. Oh, and I've also been studying sign language."

I liked the way her eyes lit up while she talked about her passions. "That's dope. But bilingual? Not you dropping a major flex like it's just small talk."

She laughed. "That's nothing huge," she said, brushing it off. "I completed the interpretation degree program at a community college and didn't do much with it. Over the past year, I've been shadowing interpreters to become more fluent and prepare for interpreting part-time."

"What made you want to learn?"

She shrugged, but I caught the way her voice softened. "Mostly due to seeing people overlooked because no one knew how to properly communicate with them. I kept wishing someone would bridge the gap; then I figured—why shouldn't I be the one who tries?"

"Have you gotten to use it in real time yet?"

"Actually, yeah," she said. "The lady I shadow, Hannah, let me step in a few times. It's... humbling. The relief I see in the eyes of the people I help... the feeling's incredible."

I nodded. "I don't doubt it. You've been changing the lives of students for years."

She smiled again. "Thanks, Rue. Showing up for people in a way that matters is my little gift to the world."

"It's far more than little. Keep going. And let me know if there's anything I can do to support you on your journey."

"Will do," she said. "So, what about your hobbies?"

"I collect watches and make cigars."

Her eyes widened. "Cigars? Seriously?"

"Yeah. Collect them too. I have a humidor at home with some rare ones. I don't even plan to smoke half of them. Same with watches. I'll admit, it's becoming an expensive problem."

"That's actually kind of sexy," she said, her voice playful. "Unexpected. Sophisticated, low-key dangerous."

"Dangerous?" I laughed, eyebrows cocked. "Maybe if you're allergic to cedar and leather."

She cackled, which caught me off guard. My dad jokes usually only earned eye rolls, especially from Cameron.

She tilted her head. "There's something about a man with muscles and tobacco. Any other hidden talents?"

"Not especially. I've been learning French in my spare time. Trying to surprise Cam with a trip to Nice one day."

"Nice?" she said, eyebrows raised. "Now, that's impressive. Most people get hung up on Paris."

Rue chuckled. "Paris is beautiful, no doubt. But Nice is where I can picture Cam. Long beach walks, fresh seafood, exploring the city. He'd love the water, and I'd love seeing him out there living free."

Tawni's smile widened, and I noticed how pretty and straight her teeth were. "That's really thoughtful of you, Rue. Handcrafting your own memorable experience for him."

I shrugged, not doing much to hide my grin. "Yeah, I'm looking forward to it. That's if I can survive city permitting offices and contractor excuses."

I immediately recognized how my comment shifted the energy. Her brow creased in concern. I couldn't help it. Tawni pulled out my desire to open up. I never felt like I was oversharing. "Work stress?"

I nodded. "The whole project's stalled. Permits, endless inspections—municipal bureaucracy's a special kind of hell. We've got crews waiting and budgets burning in real time, and it's... incredibly frustrating."

"I bet. That sounds exhausting."

"It is," I admitted. "The new crew I've been assigned is qualified for this level of work. But ever since the pandemic, it's harder to find qualified workers. Not without much higher pay. But... talking about it makes it feel a little less heavy."

She gave me a soft smile. "It will work out, Rue. Just sounds like one of those valleys before the next high."

After a few beats passed, she glanced over quickly before returning her eyes to the road.

"Is there a particular reason why you've stayed in that role?"

I rubbed a hand across my jaw, considering her loaded question. "Yeah... I asked for the hard projects."

Her brow arched a little as she tilted her head again, interest written across her face.

I continued. "Early on, I realized the firm was only chasing high-rise contracts downtown and luxury spots that saw very few people of color walking through the doors," I said, my voice low. "So I started asking for different work—youth centers, clinics, small businesses, community hubs... work that meant something to the neighborhoods that raised me."

Her grip relaxed slightly on the wheel.

"I figured if I was going to fight through red tape, it should be for things that mattered most to me—something that might still be impacting lives long after I'm gone." I paused, turning toward her. "I'm not trying to jump on a soapbox or anything. It's just a truthful answer."

Her mouth parted like she might say something, but she closed it again, and a soft, sweet smile spread across her face. I wanted to know the secret she'd tucked behind her lips. Finally, she said, "You may not be trying to impress me, Rue... but you definitely are."

"So you're saying I'm smooth with the city planning?"

She laughed, and relief flooded me. I didn't often share my real reason for the work I do with anyone other than my closest friends. I wasn't ashamed; I just didn't want it to seem performative. But Tawni wanted to know me. She was curious about my goals and what drove me. After Willow passed, I'd almost forgotten what that felt like.

"You're building spaces people need that aren't just fancy architecture, but legacy."

I nodded. Legacy. She placed emphasis on that word like she knew what it meant to me. I'd have to let her know all about it. Or maybe not. Perhaps she already did.

"Well, hopefully, you can fit in a few more moments for yourself now that Cameron's off at camp. I've been taking myself on solo dates lately—dinner, movies, even art museums. After an especially exhausting school year, I needed something that felt like *me* again."

That caught me off guard—in a good way. "I'm sorry to hear

you've had a tough school year, but it's good that you're taking that initiative. Most people avoid doing those things alone."

She shrugged. "I used to be a little self-conscious while dining alone. But I realized peace doesn't require a plus one."

"Hmm," I said. "You might be the most self-aware person I know."

She laughed, and I glanced at her just long enough to catch her lashes lower and the downward tilt of her head. We weren't even halfway to Akron, and already, I was catching glimpses of layers she probably didn't show everyone. And damn if I didn't want to keep unwrapping them.

We pulled up to the venue and parked. After I showed the attendant our mobile tickets, we entered the theater. The moment we walked into House Three Thirty—a reimagined venue owned by LeBron James—I felt the vibe shift. The lounge pulsed with laid-back, electric energy. It was all velvet seats, retro lighting, and grown-folk energy, like someone had taken the essence of an Ohio summer night and poured it into a fine cabaret glass.

Tawni and I rushed to secure prime seats right in the center, facing the stage and a makeshift dance floor—the perfect vantage point for watching grown folks get loud and loose. We slid into the cushioned velvet booth, designed for long conversations and easy laughter.

"This is a vibe," she said, scanning a menu.

I sat close enough that our legs grazed beneath the table and smiled, soaking it all in. "Yeah, I heard this is the place to be for grown folks. I was sold on the full playlist of classic R&B hits."

She smirked, eyeing me critically. "So you came to sing?"

"Oh, fa sho. I don't play about Jodeci."

"I guess we'll see about that."

The menu was all comfort food—nachos, wings, burgers,

pizza—but she ordered the crispy chicken sandwich, and I went for the ribs and fries. We ordered drinks—red wine for her, Grey Goose and cranberry for me. The food came out fast, and a few bites in, the DJ dropped a Tyrese track, and the room erupted into off-key harmonies. There was no need for lyrics on a screen or mics. We were just a crowd of happy strangers belting out 'Sweet Lady' like it was our national anthem. Some folks swayed on the dance floor. Others harmonized with their crew while seated. Birthdays, bachelorette parties, and social groups celebrated at tables along the wall. The vibe was chill, intimate, soulful, and soaked in nostalgia.

We took a few more sips, exchanged some light jokes about the crowd (and the two uncles on the floor reenacting a Boyz II Men video for a small group of unimpressed ladies).

I leaned in, my voice just above a whisper. "You wanna hit the dance floor tonight?"

"In these heels?" She glanced down at her five-inch stilettos. "Only if you promise to catch me if I fall."

"I promise to catch you, even if you don't."

That vow seemed to melt a little of her caution. She bit her lip and nodded. "Gonna take you up on that, Mr. Edwards."

When the next track transitioned into Maxwell's "Ascension," she stood, and I followed suit. On the dance floor, I stood behind her, singing into her ear with my arms resting around her waist.

Her clean, flowery scent wrapped around me as we swayed in sync. She leaned back and rested her head against my shoulder. My words, low and off-key, made her smile so wide I thought her face might split. She turned to face me slowly, letting the music guide her movements. We locked eyes, still singing and smiling. Understanding and a soft sensuality stirred between us. I read the hunger that matched mine in her round eyes.

"You were holding back at Cherry's," I said, lips barely moving.

"So were you," she replied, her tone smug.

"What are we going to do about that?"

Her breath hitched. "I... don't know yet."

Our foreheads touched, and our lips brushed, but we didn't kiss. We enjoyed toeing the line, stoking the passion between us. The song ended, but we didn't break our embrace, caught in the afterglow of a moment that felt entirely ours. Her chest rose and fell with growing speed, and my heart was hammering through my chest as I fought to even my breathing.

As people started to file out, I asked, "What are you doing to me?"

Tawni's eyes searched mine, her gaze steady. "Maybe the better question is... what are *we* doing to each other?"

I swallowed hard, feeling the question settle between us, bearing an invitation and a warning.

She ran her fingers lightly over the collar of my shirt, smoothing it out like she needed something to do with her hands. "You make me feel like I can exhale."

I wrapped my fingers gently around her wrist. "You can, as long as I'm around."

Her smile was soft, a little disbelieving, but not dismissive. "I wish it were that easy."

"I know," I said. "But I'm not asking for easiness. Only realness."

She studied me again, looking like she was trying to decide if I meant it. Then she rose up on her toes and pressed a light kiss to my cheek.

"Let's see where this goes," she whispered. "But slow, okay? I want to feel everything."

"Slow," I repeated, nodding. "I'm not in a rush."

She smiled, looping her arm through mine as we turned toward the exit and asked, "Dessert or drive home?"

"Mmm, ice cream," I said without hesitation. "The late-night kind's the best kind."

"Definitely," she said.

The heat from the lounge trailed us outside. We drove off to chase down something sweet, and I held onto her hand, refusing to break our connection. After grabbing our treats, I pulled over near Summit Lake—a quiet spot just outside the bustle of downtown. The water shimmered in the low light, and it felt like we had the whole place to ourselves. She licked her mint ice cream before it dripped off the cone. They were all out of vanilla bean, and she tried to hide her disappointment when settling for her second favorite, mint chocolate chip.

I watched her for a moment, then turned my gaze to the water. "Cam called earlier."

She looked up from her cone. "Oh yeah? How's he doing?"

"Good, mostly. Still adjusting to camp life... made some new friends, had a little drama with another kid. He handled it better than I expected." I paused, then glanced back at her. "He stood up for himself responsibly. But I'm trying to figure out the right balance between checking in and letting him work things out on his own."

Tawni gave a quiet nod but stayed silent.

"I know you worked with him," I added, studying her profile in the low light. "You probably saw things in him I couldn't... as his dad."

She hesitated, then smiled politely. "Cam's always been thoughtful. Strong-willed, but smart enough to know when to listen. You've clearly done a great job raising him."

The way she said it sounded formal. Guarded, even.

"But?" I asked, nudging gently.

She gave a soft smile, eyes still on the lake. "Wow, I don't know. I mean, it's been years since I've had Cameron in my class. You know him better than anyone," she said. "You should trust your gut on this one."

I nodded slowly. "Fair. I just... value your opinion. Always have when it comes to Cam."

She looked over at me with soft eyes. "That means a lot, Rue. Really."

I let it settle there. The last thing I wanted to do was pressure her or burden her with expectations. But it was hard to mask my disappointment.

"So..." she said, brightening her tone, "this was hands down one of the best nights I've had in a long time."

I grinned. "Even better than Cherry's Lounge?"

"So much better. Cherry's had spice, but this had soul."

"And ribs," I faked a groan while patting my stomach in satisfaction.

She laughed, bumping her shoulder against mine. "I'm going to have to get you outdoors for our next date."

I leaned in, letting the words slip before I could second-guess them. "So you're saying there *will* be a next date?"

Her lashes fluttered, but she didn't look away. "If there isn't, I might have a problem with that."

"I'd really like that. Since I planned tonight, you have the next one."

She raised a brow. "Anything I want?"

I nodded. "Anything. With no complaints from me."

Her smile was adorable with a hint of mischief. "I have to say, I can't wait to see you squirm, Mr. Edwards."

The breeze shifted, wafting faint scents of summer into the car—grass, lake water, and fertilizer. We sat in silence for a while, finishing our cones and watching the ripples skate across the lake.

"I know we just said we'd take things slow," I said, watching her from the corner of my eye, "but this feels... just like it's supposed to."

To my relief, Tawni nodded, shifting in her seat to face me. "So natural. I think we could handle it if it starts to move a little quicker."

My eyes darted to her lips as she slowly licked her ice cream cone. I didn't say it out loud, but my response echoed deep in my chest: *It's unnerving, but I'm damn sure going to try my hardest.* Judging by the way her hand found mine and lingered there, I believed she would too.

Chapter 12
Tawni

The parking lot outside Greater Community Faith & Fellowship was jumping by the time we pulled in. Row after row of folding tables lined the pavement, fresh fruit, kale chips, low-sugar granola, and other things I knew Mom would clown.

Children darted between booths toting balloon animals, while volunteers in matching royal blue T-shirts directed traffic and handed out schedules for the day's events. The temperature was high for June, and the energy gave more of a block party vibe than a health fair. But, given how Black communities can make most any event a good time, it was the norm.

"Okay," my older sister Jaclyn trilled, pulling her designer shades down as she stepped out of the back of my car. "They went all out for this one."

I grabbed my tote bag and shut the door behind her. "Yeah, this is Cleveland's biggest community outreach fair. They partner with the Hearing and Speech Center every year to contract certified interpreters. It's kind of a big deal."

I went to help Mom out of the passenger seat, but she was

already halfway up the walkway, sandals smacking the concrete like she was on an unknown mission. "I'll be at the blood pressure machine, then the prayer tents," she hollered without turning around.

I laughed and shook my head. After a health scare a couple of years back, my mother, Barbara Alexander, did not play about her wellness. I supported any behavior that kept her with us longer.

"Don't let her fool you," Jaclyn said, rolling her eyes affectionately. "She'll be at the bakery tents for them pound cake samples, too."

As we edged further into the city square, the line dancers were putting their boots on the ground, led by Patience, a line dance instructor I followed on social media. I made a mental note to join them after my shift was over. I scanned the area until I spotted Hannah, my interpreter mentor, standing near the stage.

"That's me, sis," I told Jaclyn, gesturing toward the health services tent. "I'm mostly shadowing today, but I'll jump in if Darlene needs to take a break. You can go explore. And please make sure you get your blood pressure checked along with Mom."

She waved me off like I was an annoying little sister, but I was relieved when I saw her veer right at the end of the path, toward the wellness station. I was halfway through interpreting for a vendor handing out heart health brochures when Hannah motioned for me to join her on the other side of the gazebo. I walked toward the nutrition workshop where a crowd had started to gather.

Hannah held out her arm for a side hug. "I'm so glad you could make it today, Tawni. I see you brought your family with you."

I nodded, wondering how she knew they were related to me.

Reading my expression, Hannah said, "The family resemblance is remarkable. Your mother doesn't look a day past fifty."

"Don't tell her that. She already thinks she has unlimited energy," I said. "I'm finally done with teaching summer school, so I'll have more time to pitch in this summer."

"Well, that's great because we could really use some extra hands on deck," Hannah said. She gestured toward a petite woman with passion twists, speaking to a nurse a few feet away. Her body language was tight with frustration.

"That's Yolanda," Hannah whispered. "The nurse is having a hard time explaining her dietary options to her, and I've got another person in the blood pressure tent who needs my assistance."

"Sure," I said. "I've got her."

I walked over, introducing myself to Yvonne in ASL to put her at ease. She nodded, then signed that she'd just gotten out of the hospital after a hypertensive episode. Her meds were making her dizzy, the approved food list was bland and expensive, and she felt like nobody understood what she was going through. The worry lines around her eyes showed me she was angry, tired, and disheartened.

I signed back with compassion, speaking with enunciation so she could lip-read. I focused on choosing the right words while ensuring that my face mirrored my emotions. I let her know that she wasn't alone and that I heard her. When she nodded, wiping her eyes, I turned to the nurse with calm hazel eyes.

"Hi, I'm Tawni, the assigned interpreter for this event," I said, extending my hand to her.

She shook it and said, "Hi Tawni, I'm Georgia. I'm happy to help Yvonne in any way I can."

Once I began translating between the two women, I sensed the tension easing. We all conversed for a few minutes until something shifted. Georgia fished in her bag and produced a flyer with low-sodium recipes for common dishes, and Yvonne closed her eyes, finally exhaling.

"Thank you both," she signed, pressing a hand to her heart. "Tawni, you were very helpful."

"You're so very welcome," I signed and spoke, my eyes as soft as my voice. "We're here for you. Please reach out if you need any other assistance with diet maintenance or supporting your new lifestyle."

When Yvonne walked away, I noticed Jaclyn standing nearby with her arms crossed tightly over her chest. Her lips were pressed together like she was holding something in. I walked over to her and we began heading toward a shady pillar. She handed me a fruit skewer and a cold bottled water.

"Thanks, sis," I said, immediately screwing off the top and taking a long sip.

She leaned against the brick wall and stared out over the lot.

"That woman," she said after a few moments, "Yvonne. She was hospitalized because of high blood pressure?"

"That's what she said," I said, biting into a pineapple chunk. "She doesn't have much support, and things just got overwhelming for her. It happens more than you'd think."

When Jaclyn didn't respond right away, I knew I'd struck a nerve.

"I'm not trying to nag," I said, keeping my tone gentle. "But it's why I wanted you to join me today."

She sighed and finally looked at me. "Seeing her like that shook me. She looked like she's been desperately trying to hold everything together."

I nodded. "And maybe she has. But she showed up today. That counts for something."

Jaclyn puffed up her cheeks before saying, "Okay. Here's what I can commit to. Walking at least three times a week. As long as you keep doing this interpreter thing. Because I can see the difference you're making."

I turned to face her. My sister wasn't normally liberal with compliments or praise. It felt good to know her thoughts on the work I was doing. "This work gives me purpose. So many people with health issues want to change their lives, but they're fighting the battle all alone."

She nodded. "I definitely feel that. But for me, it's not a lack of support. It's stubbornness."

I took another sip of my water and nodded, knowing better than to agree with her.

After pausing for a moment, Jaclyn slid her sunglasses up into her curls. "So... what's going on with your love life, lil sis? You got any prospects yet so you can get over Dante and move on with your life?"

The question came out casually, but it was the bite underneath that got to me. After forcing a smile and taking another sip of water, I replied, "Actually... I've been seeing someone."

Jaclyn blinked. "Since when?"

"It's new." I kept my voice even. "His name's Rue."

She angled her head toward me like a hawk zeroing in. "Is that short for something?"

"Rudolph, but he just goes by Rue."

"So what's Rudolph's story? Where'd you meet him?"

I hid an eye roll as I bit into another pineapple chunk, chewing slowly. "I had his son in my class several years ago."

"Tawni. This sounds messy as hell."

"It's not. He's a widower and a great father."

The silence that followed stretched on too long for me to ignore. "Just speak your mind, Jaclyn."

"So, you're dating a man with a child *and* a deceased wife? Tawn, I ask this with love, but are you ready to take on all that?"

I kept my expression blank while my stomach flipped.

"That's a lot to carry," she continued. "You're already a natural caretaker, and I worry that you'll get pulled into being a stand-in mama or an emotional crutch for a man who's still healing. You don't do casual well. You never have."

I forced another sip of water as I fought back the choice words bubbling in my chest. "Jac, I really appreciate your concern. But, respectfully, I've got this."

Her skepticism seasoned the air between us. I knew my sister meant well, but her doubt never failed to hit, bringing additional weight that I hadn't asked to take on.

"Look, Tawni," Jaclyn finally said, her voice lowering. "You've really grown since breaking up with Dante. You're stronger and more sure of yourself and you're not hiding who you are anymore. I just don't want to see you lose all that progress."

I blinked, unsure if I was more surprised by the softness in her tone or everything she'd noticed.

"Sister," she continued, "I'm not saying this to pick at you. But I've seen you dim your light for men—over and over again. Tiptoeing past their moods, shrinking yourself, trying not to make waves."

She turned to face me. "I don't want you to step into another relationship where you end up carrying someone else's responsibility to heal on your back. Especially not a grieving man with a whole child. That's heavy, and I know how easily you put yourself last."

Bit by bit, her words painfully sliced through my quiet

confidence like a dull blade. I kept my cool, but internally, I tensed. Although I didn't like how she'd instantly chosen to see Rue as a liability instead of the incredible man he was, I knew her concerns weren't completely wrong.

I hadn't intentionally started this connection with Rue, and I certainly didn't walk into our first date expecting to carry his past—or anyone else's. But Jaclyn's words still struck a nerve. They weren't cruel, but they echoed a fear I hadn't let myself say out loud and stirred up questions I hadn't fully allowed myself to face.

What if I was doing it again?

What if the possibility of something new with Rue—no matter how tender or promising—was still just my way of dissolving into someone else's life and calling it my own?

"Anyway, that's all I have to say about that," Jaclyn, said, waving her hand dismissively. "So, we'll check in with each other about sticking to our goals?"

I was still stuck in the mental whirlwind her words had created, but I'd have ti process my thoughts about it later. Today was about being with my family and I didn't want to ruin the moment. Grinning, I held out my pinky. "Definitely. Now, put it on Scrappy."

She rolled her eyes at my reference to her childhood toy bunny that she still had to this day. She linked her pinky with mine. "Why do you always have to be so extra with it?."

"Coming from the woman with a full face of Fenty at a health fair."

"And what? My next husband may be here."

"And you're going to scare his ass away with your face melting like that," I said, fanning her with my napkin.

We both cracked up just as Mom returned, clutching her to-go box to her chest.

"Ladies," she said, smiling with her whole face. "Y'all ready to hit up that healthy soul food truck before we head out?"

Jaclyn and I exchanged glances before nodding simultaneously with an enthusiasm we hadn't shared since middle school. I followed Jaclyn toward the smell of grilled salmon, steamed veggies, and hot water cornbread, grateful for the peace between us. I snuck a glance at Mom, who studied us carefully, her eyes shining as if she'd won the lottery, and that was enough to make the whole day worth it.

Chapter 13
Tawni

I was in my second-favorite sanctuary. The hum of hair dryers, the smell of freshly pressed hair, and Viv's gentle humming soothed me as I sat in her salon chair. It had been almost a year since my last appointment—long enough to forget how much I'd missed this place, and even longer since I'd taken time for myself in this way.

"I'm so glad to see you. Girl, I thought you'd moved or gotten kidnapped," Viv said with a grin as she tied the cape around my neck.

"Yeah, it's been a minute," I sighed. "Life's been... a lot lately."

Viv clicked her tongue and parted my hair, examining my roots with the ease of a seasoned pro. "You and me both. Catch me up. How are things with the job? How's Dante?"

I tensed. For a half-second, I considered brushing past her question just so I wouldn't have to keep talking about him. But the innocent curiosity in her voice disarmed me. Viv wasn't messy. She wasn't on social media either, so she didn't realize she was revisiting a chapter I'd already closed—multiple times.

"I wouldn't know," I said finally. "We broke up last spring."

Viv paused, comb in mid-air. "What?"

"Yep," I said, keeping my tone even.

Viv blinked. "Damn, I'm sorry, Tawni. Y'all were together for a minute. What happened?"

I hesitated. At first, the irritation bubbled up. I was tired of Dante popping up when he was no longer invited in my life. But as I sat there, weighing how many details to share during this very public conversation, I decided it wasn't worth trying to keep things under wraps. Viv had always supported our relationship, so I would tell her whatever she wanted to know.

I exhaled. "It wasn't working," I said finally. "I made it seem like things were fine, but he wasn't good to me. Not in the ways that matter most."

Viv stopped combing. "Wait, what do you mean? He seemed so—"

"Put together? Polished? Charming?" I offered with a tight smile. "Yeah. He was all of that. Especially when other people were watching."

I watched Viv's eyes soften in the mirror, concern replacing her curiosity.

"He had this way of tearing me down, but in increments. Little things, like repeatedly correcting me in front of our friends or making jabs behind the thin veil of jokes." I paused. "He made me feel small. Kept me on my toes like I was always one misstep away from being replaced."

"Damn," she said, shaking her head.

"It chipped away at me over time. I stopped recognizing myself. Stopped speaking up. I thought if I just worked harder or loved him better, he'd stop looking at me like I wasn't enough." My throat tightened, but I pushed through. "We were together for three years. And when it finally ended, it wasn't even because of a fight. It was because he made it clear I was never going to be who he wanted. And I stopped trying."

Viv blinked slowly, her eyes glistening. "Tawn..."

"I'm okay," I said, offering her a small smile. "Really. I've done the hard work—therapy, late-night crying sessions, and I even took some solo vacations. But seeing him move on so fast," I scoffed, "and proposing to her like what we had was nothing? It messed with my head. Made me question everything."

Viv stiffened as if stunned by the news of the engagement. Then she gently placed her hands on my shoulders. "Yeah. I've been there. That kind of heartbreak is tricky as shit because it rewrites memories. You start wondering if maybe it wasn't as bad as you remember..."

"Exactly," I said. "Like, maybe I was the damn problem. Maybe I was tripping. Could I have overreacted? But then I really get to thinking and it all comes back—clear as day. I remember feeling like I had to shrink myself just to keep the peace. And no matter how fast he jumped into his next love story, it had nothing to do with me. I finally set a boundary, and he paid the price for crossing it."

Viv squeezed my shoulder. "That's real, Tawn. I hate that you went through that. But I'm proud of you for getting out. And for talking about it. I know it's not easy."

"Thanks," I whispered, blinking fast to hold back tears.

Viv nodded and handed me a tissue. She said in a low voice, "I think you just needed to hear yourself say it."

I smiled faintly, looking at my reflection. My curls were long—stretched from stress, breakage, and years of me being too busy to give them proper care.

"I'm not who I was when I was with him," I said. "Not even close."

"Damn right."

"And I don't want to look like her anymore, either. Cut this shit off."

Viv's brows arched so high I thought they'd touch her head-wrap. "Harpo, who dis woman?"

"Still me," I said with a smile. "Just more certain about what I want."

Viv clapped her hands. "Okay then. So we'll match that energy on your head."

"I want a pixie. Short-short. Jet black with subtle bronze highlights," I said, rushing my words before I could talk myself out of it.

Viv grinned like she was envisioning those snipping shears. "Oh, I see you tryna be *that* girl this summer. I just got this bold new color line and I've been itching to try it."

"Let's do it."

After sectioning my hair, she grabbed her shears. "We'll cut first, then color. Ready?"

I nodded, and sat up straighter, heart thumping. This was it.

The first snip was quiet. A test. A thick lock of hair fell and slid down the cape. After pausing for a moment, she continued. One by one, the pieces fell: curls that had clung to heartache, history, and habit. Each strand that hit the cape felt like an emotional release.

Viv caught my gaze in the mirror. "You good?"

Realizing I'd been holding my breath, I exhaled hard and nodded again. "Keep going, Viv."

With each curl that dropped, a strange mixture of emotions washed over me: nerves, yes—but excitement, too. Freedom. The final snip felt like a punctuation mark. A full stop on who I used to be.

As Viv painted the bronze and blended in the golden high-lights, we caught up on everything from teacher burnout to

TikTok recipes gone wrong. I told her about my solo brunches and quiet walks through botanical gardens, about the way I'd started reading poetry again and fell back in love with it.

Viv led me to the shampoo bowl. As she massaged my scalp, all the tension from the past few weeks—work stress, canceled plans, the ghost of Dante—melted away and slipped down the drain. My eyes fluttered closed.

"You ready for this?" she asked, towel-wrapping my hair as we made our way back to her station.

"I think so." My voice barely rose above a whisper.

I gripped the armrests as she removed the towel. Gasping quietly, I kept my eyes trained on the mirror. She watched me closely as she spritzed my hair, then blow-dried it. I didn't breathe a word as she styled the soft black strands. It wasn't until she rubbed oil on her hands and pulled the final strands of my pixie that I noticed the copper highlights shimmering in the overhead lights. I barely recognized myself. My reflection was bold, bright, and soft all at once. And beneath the nerves, I felt power inside of me that had been lying dormant.

"Rue's gonna love this," I muttered, running fingers through it.

"Rue, you say?" Viv asked, tilting her head forward while lifting a brow.

I laughed. "Yes. It's new. And I kinda like him," I admitted. "I think that's what makes it scary. I don't want to lose myself again."

She gently parted my hair. "Do you think wanting love and keeping yourself are mutually exclusive?"

"I used to." I swallowed. "Now I'm a little scared I still do."

She didn't say anything at first. Sectioned my hair and looked at me through the mirror.

"Maybe the work isn't choosing between the two," she said

finally, "but learning how to love someone without disappearing."

That hit. So hard, I couldn't respond for a while. Nodding, I drifted away with my thoughts, her flat iron smoothing out my hair reminding me I was still there.

"Wondering what he'll think is usually the good kind of scary," Viv said as she smoothed the back of my hair. "It always shows up after you've finally made space for something better. So, will he like it? He will," Viv said confidently. "But more importantly, *you do*."

She was right. I paid her and stepped down from the chair. I almost jumped when the room erupted in a wave of cheers, applause, and whistles.

"Okay, Bronze Bombshell!"

"You ownin' that color, sis."

"She in her soft girl era!"

I laughed, a little overwhelmed by sheer joy. And then, I couldn't help but give them what they came for. I broke into a slow, confident Naomi Campbell strut through the salon, hips swaying, legs pushing forward under my flowy sundress, cheekbones sitting high, eyes fixed ahead like the red carpet was waiting for me outside.

I opened the door to the sound of a few final catcalls and a stylist shouting, "Tell your bummy ex he fumbled the hell out of this one!"

Grinning, I didn't look back. I was no longer thinking about him or even who I was an hour ago.

It was far more rewarding to focus on the woman I'd just committed to becoming.

Chapter 14
Rudolph

When half my team calls off and my subcontractor misses another deadline, I always know it's Monday morning. I was on my feet before I even had a chance to pour my morning coffee. Site issues. Delayed deliveries. The permits still hadn't cleared, which meant the demo crew I booked last week had to be rescheduled for the third time. Chase, my new project coordinator, had the audacity to show up forty minutes late with a smoothie in hand, like he was casually late to brunch.

"Hey, Rudolph! Sorry, traffic was crazy."

I sighed. I'd corrected him three times already—*call me Rue.* Nobody called me Rudolph except my mom when she was heated, and even then, it came with a lecture and a pointed finger. But Chase was one of those people who didn't listen unless you wrote it in bold and stapled it to his forehead.

"You live eleven minutes from the site," I said, my tone flatter than a flapjack. "Don't insult both of us."

He stammered, offered a weak laugh, then scurried off.

I rubbed the bridge of my nose and pulled out my phone to

check emails. That was my mistake. I was bombarded with notifications for seventeen unread messages, five voicemails, and three flagged invoices.

By noon, I was deep in the thick of it—barking on phone calls, redirecting crews, and reviewing blueprints while simultaneously scarfing down a lunch I didn't remember ordering. Was I efficient? Yes. Sharp and focused? Absolutely. But I was also one wrong look away from snapping someone's head clean off.

The job paid well, but it also took its pound of flesh. Being a lead project manager meant I was everyone and their mama's sounding board, therapist, and primary emergency contact. I was the guy who fixed the things no one else wanted to deal with. That authority had gotten me pretty far, but it had also hardened me. I had no choice but to be exacting. Not cold—but colder than I would normally be. But I always showed up for my team, for Cam, and for myself. And that's what mattered most.

Around four, I finally had a moment to sit at my desk in peace. I closed my eyes, leaned back in my chair, and considered canceling the last hour of my day. Maybe I could call in sick tomorrow. I kept hearing the rest of the world use the term "personal day." I could really use one of those.

My phone buzzed loud and hard, scooting across my desk. I looked down at the screen.

Tawni: Just confirmed our date for Thursday evening. Bring your walking shoes, shades, and sunscreen.

My lips spread into a wide smile before I even realized it. My tense back loosened along with my jaw. Nothing about the day had changed, yet everything had.

Me: You got it. I'm looking forward to it.

Tawni: I can't wait to see how you handle the great outdoors.

Me: If I pass out halfway through, just drag me under a tree and tell Cam I tried.

I was physically and mentally drained, yet buzzing from what I could only describe as *the Tawni effect*.

* * *

That evening, I met up with Dorian for our semi-regular Monday night bowling sessions. He was already waiting at our usual lane, two beers in, tossing his ball with lazy precision.

"Took you long enough, Edwards," he called without looking.

"My bad, bruh. Long day."

"Clearly. You look like somebody canceled Christmas on your ass... on Christmas Eve."

I smirked, pulling my bowling shoes and custom-drilled ball out of my bag. "Don't start."

We played in easy silence for a few frames. Dorian never needed filler words. He just read the room and got it. After a few missed spares—his, not mine—he finally said, "You said it's been a long day, but you're over there grinning like a man with secrets. It's weird."

I said nothing, pretending to be focused on the 7-10 split in front of me.

Once I hit the pin on the right-hand side and returned to my seat, Dorian said, "So... tell me about her."

I raised a brow, stunned by his candor. "Who her? Her who?"

He shook his head, and we had a stare-off.

"Alright, man," Dorian said, slightly raising his hands in surrender. "I'll just wait until you're ready."

We played a few more rounds, trash talked, and cracked jokes. We were a brotherhood that didn't require explaining.

But right after his third gutter ball in a row, Dorian plopped down beside me with a sigh and took a long sip of his beer.

"Man, to be honest... some days still catch me off guard," he said, eyes fixed on the neon score screen. "Like I'll see something random and funny, and I'll be waiting for her to call me to laugh about it."

I glanced at him and nodded. "Yeah. Happens to me too, bro. All the time." My voice was so low, it was almost swallowed by the crashing pins.

For a moment, neither of us moved. The sounds of rolling balls and low music from the snack bar hummed around us.

"You good for real, though?" he asked, finally turning toward me.

I shrugged, rolling my shoulder to ease the creeping tension. "I'm managing."

Dorian shook his head. "You're trying to carry far too much on your own. You stay doing that, bro."

I exhaled, rubbing my forehead. "Honestly, it's hard to know where to even set it all down."

"I'm here, Rue. Not just where Cam's involved. For whatever you need."

I nodded, grateful for the reminder that I didn't have to shoulder everything on my own.

After we wrapped up our last game, Dorian tossed his bowling shoes into his duffel and said, "Oh—almost forgot. Once camp is over, I wanna grab Cam for a week for some quality unc-neph time, as Willow always called it."

I nodded, thrown by how casually he'd said it. Dorian wasn't just family—he was Willow's twin and closest confidant. I looked forward to our time together. Our bond strengthened while managing the pain the world doesn't prepare you for. We were two people bonded forever, simply because we survived it together.

"Thanks, man. He'll love that," I said.

Dorian nodded. "All right, I'll text you. Stay up, brother."

We dapped each other up, and I hung back, sitting with my thoughts as I watched him leave.

As the door swung closed behind Dorian, I sat in stillness, the scattered noise and laughter fading into the background. Grief didn't tug at me as sharply tonight due to my work stress being at the forefront of my mind. Instead, it rested quietly beside me, and for once, I didn't feel completely alone in it. I was still figuring things out, but I was finally coming to terms with something I'd resisted for a long time: my village had been there, waiting to help me carry it all along.

* * *

We pulled into the Holden Arboretum just after ten on Saturday morning. The sun was already blazing overhead, and golden rays peeked out from behind the treetops. Tawni slid out of the car, her black designer shades catching the sunlight, and her new hairstyle sculpted to highlight every soft angle of her face. Her camera was slung across her chest over a flowy top and—my favorite—black biker shorts. Looking at her lean over and stretch her legs was the only thing keeping my nerves from running off with my sanity.

"Don't worry," she said, reading my anxious expression. "We'll ease into the activities. No five-mile hikes... today."

I chuckled, still not entirely at ease. The truth was, I'd read about the arboretum's main attractions, and I wasn't a fan of heights. But something about Tawni's excitement made it hard to say no to anything she suggested. And if anyone was going to push me outside of my comfort zone, it would be her. She made every moment of discomfort well worth it.

We started with the canopy walk, a 500-foot-long bridge

suspended 65 feet above ground. After we climbed the steps, Tawni took off for the bridge. I took a few deep breaths to calm my raging nerves, then took my first timid step. The wooden plank creaked slightly beneath my weight, and I averted my gaze from the scary view beneath me that plunged straight to the forest floor. With each step, I was painfully aware of how the canopy swayed and bounced. But when I looked to my left, the view was unreal—like we were walking through the uppermost layer of a living, breathing painting. The trees rustled beneath us, birds darted through the branches, and the warm sunlight filtered down in radiant waves.

When I finally caught up with Tawni, she was snapping photos of the wildflowers peeking through the leaves. She looked completely in her element, energized by the serene landscape surrounding us.

"Isn't this incredible?" she breathed, turning back to look at me. "I can't believe we've both lived in Northeast Ohio our whole lives and haven't been here before."

"Yeah, this place is calming. I'm starting to think I've been missing out on a lot," I said, steadying myself as I followed her across a narrow portion of the bridge. "What else do you have in store for me?"

She smirked. "Wouldn't you like to know?"

We made it through the canopy walk without incident, other than sweaty palms. I wasn't ashamed to admit my knuckles had a death grip on the rail for most of it. Tawni didn't make a big deal out of my nerves; she just stayed steady, which helped me move at my own pace. I was pretty proud of myself for pushing through—until we reached the emergent tower. The attraction stood 120 feet tall, looking like something out of an adventure movie—spiraling stairs enclosed in a metal cage, leading out to a lookout deck.

"This one has panoramic views of Lake Erie. You ready?" Tawni asked, her hand resting lightly on my arm.

"Define ready," I muttered.

She laughed. "Come on. We'll take it slow."

With every step up the spiraling staircase, my heart thumped harder. I focused on my breathing, kept my eyes straight ahead, and tried not to picture plummeting to the forest floor. Tawni stayed close, cracking jokes to distract me. But I felt each of those 202 steps. Every single one.

When we reached the top, I had to take a moment to get myself together.

"Still with me?" she asked, slipping her hand into mine.

"Barely," I admitted, squeezing her fingers and stepping out onto the platform.

The canopy swayed gently in the breeze, and I cautiously edged to the railing. The view stopped me cold. Endless greenery stretched in every direction—oak, maple, and beech trees bursting with dense, fresh leaves in every shade of green. Off in the distance, the lake shimmered and rolled in gentle waves.

"You did it," she said, beaming at me with a smile that disarmed me. She held an arm out for a side hug.

"That was the longest climb of my life, but this view definitely makes it worth it," I said, placing an arm around her shoulder as we gazed out at the breathtaking kaleidoscope of nature that spread out before us.

Tawni removed her sunglasses and lifted her camera. My eyes scanned the horizon, and calmness overtook me. The moment felt sacred. We were alone up there, gazing at the 360-degree view of miles of nature, and I felt like we'd found a hidden corner of the world meant just for us.

The wind whipped Tawni's shirt, giving me a glimpse of

her sports bra underneath. I looked away for a moment as she zoomed in for another shot.

"This might be my new favorite place," she said after a few moments.

"It's up there for me as well," I said, meaning it. "Thanks for suggesting this. I can't remember the last time I've experienced such serenity."

Tawni sighed. "Yeah, I needed this. The tranquility reminds me there's so much more to life than tests, lesson plans, and metrics."

I nodded. "I've been on the same page lately. Work's been on overdrive, and even with Cam at camp, I've been anxious about what's next."

"We're not made to live like that," she said, glancing over. "That kind of pressure isn't healthy or sustainable."

I met her gaze. "We should definitely hold each other accountable to unplug more often. Starting with just once a week—every week this summer—we each need to do something just for ourselves. No excuses."

Her eyes lit up. "Are you serious? I love that idea."

"Dead-ass."

She stuck out her hand. "Don't even try to back out of this, Rue."

"Not a chance."

We smiled, shaking on it. It felt like the beginning of intentionality between us. Like we weren't just getting to know each other but actively creating a life that made space for our individual joy as well.

On the walk back down, silence rested easy between us. Everything important had already been said. And with every step we took, I felt lighter and more hopeful now that I had a partner I could rely on.

Chapter 15
Tawni

I slipped into the Cleveland Hearing and Speech Center just before class started. My mentor, Ms. Karr, had asked me to help out in her classroom because her assistant had another obligation. She was already inside, greeting students with a wide smile.

"Good evening, everyone," she called out, then signed it.

After years of leading my own classroom, it felt strange to sit on the other side of the desk among the class.

"I'm so glad you're here," she said, tapping my arm lightly as I passed her. "You'll be working with Elise tonight. She's a little shy, but I think she'll open up to you."

I nodded before taking my seat at the back of the classroom. During the breakout groups, I guided Elise and a few others through fingerspelling drills. Elise stumbled a few times but smiled when I encouraged her. "You've got this," I signed. "Take it one letter at a time."

This was why I loved teaching. Watching that click when someone found their rhythm was satisfying, but combining it with ASL lit a new spark in me. Every movement, expression, and sign was more than just language; it was connection and power.

My phone buzzed during break. I looked down to see a new message from Rue.

Rue: Hey, Teach. Just finished a run with Cam. He ran circles around me, but I held my own. No excuses.

He sent a selfie. I shifted in my seat, unprepared for what I saw. He was sweaty, smiling, and looking like a prize trophy.

Me: Looking great. What's for dinner?

Rue: A chef salad with grilled chicken breast.

Me: Okay, I see you trying. You'll be cock diesel in no time.

Rue: Gotta look my best if I'm gonna be standing next to you.

I bit back a smile. He'd promised to take better care of himself, and he was following through. It impressed me more than I expected.

When class resumed, Ms. Karr had us run emotional transition drills. She caught my eye after I helped Elise sign a short dialogue with real emotion behind it.

"You're a natural at this," she told me later. "You teach with your heart. Not everyone can."

Her praise hit deeper than any evaluation she ever could have given me. I realized I didn't have to choose between teaching and interpreting. I could do both while building something entirely new. I wanted to help other women be heard. Loud and clear. In every language. It felt good that someone else saw the work I was doing. I was headed in the right direction.

* * *

Muted lighting added to the intimate hush as I walked into *The Copper Cork*, a new cozy upscale wine bar on the east side. A lo-fi chill tune drifted from the speakers, pairing perfectly with the clinking of stemware and the low hum of conversation in the open space. I spotted my girls at a high-top table near the back and already felt myself unwinding.

"Ohhhh, okay, new woman alert!" Trish called out as I crossed the room toward them.

Tiff looked up from her phone, and her eyes went wide. She halfway stood, then plopped right back into her seat. "Tawni Alexander! Heifa, you cut your hair and didn't tell us?"

I laughed, giving each of them a hug before sliding onto my stool. "It was a last-minute thing."

"No, ma'am. You don't just wake up wanting that glow and a fresh shape-up," Trish said, pulling me back onto my feet and twirling me in a full circle. "Giving all this *main character energy* while going Toni Braxton circa '93 on us."

"I just wanted to try something different, that's all," I said, smoothing my hand over the nape of my neck, which was now nearly bare.

Tiff motioned toward me with a fake scowl. "Tawni, you look *stunning*—like 'I have secrets and a new man' stunning."

I shook my head, grinning as the server set down a flight of rosés in front of me. "Y'all are ridiculous."

"Nope. Just observant," Trish said. "And I know that look. Spill."

I raised an eyebrow over the rim of my glass. "Spill what?"

Trish smirked. "Cute. But cut the shit, Tawni."

"What's going on with you and Rue?" Tiff asked, not missing a beat. "You're slow to text back in the group chat. We suddenly have to schedule plans with you weeks in advance. Now you strut in here looking like Angela Bassett in *Waiting to Exhale. We need details, bitch.*"

I paused, twirling the stem of my glass between my fingers. For some reason, my heart rate quickened a little. It wasn't from embarrassment, but... my friends weren't wrong. I barely recognized myself these days. Exhaling, I crossed my leg and leaned in.

They mimicked my movement, eyes dancing with anticipation.

"Okay, yes. Something's been going on with me. But it's not easy to put a finger on it."

"Why not?" Trish asked. "It's obviously Rue. He's fine, attentive, successful, and most importantly—he looked at you like you were the answer to all his problems."

That made me smile, soft and slow. "All facts," I said. "And, girl, it feels... damn good. It's like I can exhale and not be on guard all the time."

Tiff elbowed Trish. "Exhale. Told you. Definitely giving Angela... *after the driveway bonfire.*"

When Trish nodded, they each stared at me for a moment. Then Trish prompted, "But?"

I looked down at my glass, watching the wine catch the light. "I'm a little nervous that I'll start getting comfortable and fall back into old habits. I just started choosing myself again."

They each nodded, waiting for me to finish.

"With Dante, it didn't happen all at once. I didn't even notice I was shrinking until I was standing in front of a mirror and barely recognized myself." I swallowed a lump hardened in my throat. "Now that I've finally started to feel like myself again... giving someone else room in my life... feels a little scarier than I thought."

"But you're not her anymore," Trish said gently. "That version of Tawni would never have cut her hair or done anything new and bold without checking in with her girls first."

Tiff nodded. "And you're not choosing Rue instead of yourself. You're choosing him *with* your new self."

I smiled, allowing their words to settle. They always knew

exactly what to say. Saw the things I couldn't quite see in myself. "It's nice dating someone who sees me as I am. Who roots for me and makes me laugh. Rue has been giving me space and challenging me to create more room for myself. That type of shit is unheard of."

"You're right about that," Trish said, shaking her head. "These dudes be straight smothering ya girl."

After side-eyeing her, Tiff lifted her glass. "Here's to more of that. Because if it has you out here looking and feeling like this—the Tawni we haven't seen since high school—then I'm rooting for Tawni 2.0!"

"And let's hear it for our boy, Rue. Not threatened by growth and ready to hold her purse while she glows the fuck up in this new era," Trish added.

Chuckling, I lifted mine too, clinking gently with theirs. "To choosing ourselves and the people who make room for who we're becoming."

As we sipped, my eyes drifted across the bar, soaking in the moment with gratitude and glee—until they landed on the last person I expected to see.

Dante. My nose wrinkled.

Typical. Dude's always been a walking vibe killer.

He was in a corner booth all hugged up tight with his fiancée. I caught the glint on her left hand resting delicately on his chest. The way his arm rested across her shoulders, how their heads tipped back in unison with laughter lighting up their faces. I wasn't happy to share space with him, but I also wasn't affected by it. I sipped my wine with measured calm and kept my gaze fixed on the girls. Thankfully, their backs were to him. Trish wasn't looking at her phone anymore—she was watching me instead, her expression soft with concern.

"We saw them walk in a few minutes before you," she said gently.

Tiff added, "You said you didn't want to talk about him anymore, and we wanted to respect that."

"But I'm glad he got a front-row seat to you walking in here serving up all that Halle Berry goodness," Trish chuckled.

I laughed and said, "I appreciate that, guys. And I meant what I said: he's now a non-factor and I've moved on. Honestly, I'm glad he's been able to do the same."

Still, something in me wanted to make it plain—if not for him, then for me.

"I'll be right back," I told the girls, setting down my glass.

Trish raised an eyebrow. "You sure?"

"Completely."

I walked across the bar with steady steps and a lifted chin, the tap of my heels purposeful. As I neared the booth, Dante looked up first, and for a brief second, his easy laughter faltered. His fiancée followed his gaze, her bright smile dimming with polite curiosity.

I smiled gently. "Hi, Dante. I just wanted to say congratulations on your engagement."

He blinked, caught off guard. "Oh. Uh... thanks, Tawni."

I turned to the woman beside him. "And congratulations to you too. Wishing you both all the best."

Her smile warmed. "That's really sweet of you, Tawni. Thank you."

"You're welcome," I said, nodding once. "Enjoy your evening."

Then I turned and walked away without a backward glance. I was comforted by a quiet satisfaction of knowing that my peace wasn't something he could rattle anymore.

By the time I reached the table, the girls had each gathered themselves, recovering from the initial shock of my bold move.

"Handled it like the grown-ass woman you are," Tiff said, sipping her wine.

I smirked, picking up my glass. "Who knew emotional evolution looked this damn good?"

Trish grinned. "Oh, we certainly did."

Our night returned to laughter, stories, and unshakable joy —the kind that doesn't ask for permission or explanation. The kind that roots itself in healing.

And I knew, without question, I was ready for whatever came next.

Chapter 16
Tawni

After having lunch at a charming little bistro with a live jazz band, neither of us wanted the date to end. Rue managed to guilt me into going for a walk afterward, and honestly, I was glad he didn't cave to my complaints about the wrong sandals or the rising temperature. The summer air was thick and warm, slowing our stroll into an easy, unhurried rhythm.

The city buzzed with a lazy energy. Couples sipped iced lattes at sidewalk tables, murals burst across brick walls, and laughter trailed a group of kids whizzing by on electric scooters.

"You ever think about leaving Cleveland?" I asked, side-stepping a couple of cyclists drifting past us.

Rue glanced at me. "As in... relocate?"

I nodded. "Sometimes I wonder what it'd be like to start fresh in a new city with new faces."

He let the thought hang for a beat. "That sounds good until you realize whatever you're running from is booking that flight right with you."

I laughed, shaking my head. "I can't argue with that."

"I've learned a few things over the years," he said with a grin that lit up his entire face. "Healing doesn't come from burying yourself in work or distractions, so changing your zip code won't help much either."

We passed a thrift shop, an old bookstore, and a bakery with rows of lemon bars in the window. Rue reached out and grabbed my hand. "Nope. We just had those big healthy salads. If you grab a couple, I'll grab no less than six, claiming I'm getting some from Cam. Then none of them will make it home."

I laughed. We kept walking for a few minutes until I stopped cold in front of a wide windowpane with vivid art displayed throughout the display.

"Wait. I think my friend came here for an acrylic pour painting class. She couldn't stop talking about how great the staff is."

Rue followed my gaze. "Is it a small business?"

"Yeah," I said, stepping closer to peer inside. "They do all kinds of freestyle activities. One of them is paint throwing. It's like therapy."

Rue tilted his head, gesturing to his fresh Air Forces. "You're trying to throw paint on these, Teach?"

I smirked. "That won't happen... if you can dodge it."

He pulled the shop door open with a shrug. "Let's find out."

Inside, the air was cooler and quieter. The front of the shop was cozy and clean, with rows of finished canvases lining the walls and an old record player humming Erykah Badu in the corner. A woman in overalls and stylish glasses looked up from a counter, smiling like we were right on time.

"Welcome in. First time here?" she asked warmly.

I waved and said, "Yes. I've been meaning to stop in."

"So glad you made it in today. Are you here to paint? The paint room is free."

"Oh, we weren't planning—" I started.

Rue jumped in. "Actually, we're curious."

The woman's grin widened. "Then I have to show y'all around. A Bible study group just cleared out, so it'll be quiet now. You look like you could use a little... creative chaos."

We exchanged a look. Rue's handsome features lit up with curiosity. I was half sold already, but keeping it cool.

The woman waved us toward the back. "Come see this splatter room. People walk in tense and leave relaxed with a dope memento to show for it."

Rue leaned in close, his breath brushing my ear as we followed her. "That maxi dress—how it's hugging you in all the right places—has me a little tense right now."

Heat crawled up the side of my neck. His voice was low and deliberate, like he knew exactly what it would do to me. And the way he emphasized the word *tense*... my pulse caught an off-beat rhythm and I bit the inside of my cheek. This was the first time Rue had been so direct in expressing the effect I had on him. I'd always felt the sexual tension—those prolonged stolen glances, lingering touches—but this was different. It wasn't playful or vague. It was intentional. And how much I liked it made me a little nervous.

I stepped into the splatter paint room first. He trailed me, looking around like a kid sneaking through a portal into a secret new world. The space was narrow and industrial with exposed brick walls stained in dozens of chaotic colors—neon greens, fuchsia, indigo, and burnt orange. The floor was a constellation of footprints, paint globs, and a beautiful mix of mayhem. A canvas on an easel dared us to give it our best shot. A utility cart overflowed like a painter's war chest.

Rue looked around and let out a low whistle. "This place has seen some real shit."

"And more tragic breakups than a Taylor Swift album," I added, shaking my head.

The woman laughed. "So, are you game?"

"You have protective gear?" I asked.

"Full suits, gloves, goggles, and shoe covers."

Rue was already rubbing his hands and grinning like a kid on Christmas. I nodded. "Let's do it."

Suited up, we stepped inside. It was intimate, with just enough room for two. I grabbed a bottle of gold, my favorite color. Rue picked up a teal and white.

Three minutes in, the canvas, ceiling, walls, and floors were covered in new colorful streaks, dots, and splotches.

I squealed, narrowly dodging his flying paint missile. "Why do I love this so much?"

"This is the first time in a while that something I've done didn't have to come out perfect," Rue said, wiping his brow and inadvertently smudging more paint across his forehead. "We get to just throw it out there and see what sticks."

I stilled. He wasn't just talking about paint.

"Speaking of things sticking," I said, grabbing lavender, "I had my second observation for the ASL mentorship program last night. It went really well."

Rue raised his brows, impressed. "That's good. You're almost done, right?"

"Three more sessions. Then I'll lead my own team at community events, job fairs, and medical centers."

"That's major, Tawni," he said, his voice dipping low. "You're about to make a real impact."

"It feels good," I said. "I've wanted to do this for so long. Now I get to do it on my own terms."

Rue looked at me. "I love that for you."

We held the moment. I held his eyes for another beat, hoping for more.

He cleared his throat. "Cam comes home from his uncle's next week. I've been planning our first couple of days. Nothing too heavy—just space for him to talk."

"That's smart," I said, squeezing a dollop of yellow paint onto my glove and dotting it in the corners of the canvas. "Is he looking forward to coming home?"

"Yeah. Camp was good, but that quiet confidence he's learned to project feels like a veneer. Sometimes he glosses over the hard stuff."

I nodded, wiping my hands and looking over at him. "You think something happened?"

He told me Cameron had an issue with another camper who was bullying others.

"I hate he had to go through that," I said. "But camps have a zero-tolerance bullying policy like schools. You'll know what to ask when he's ready to talk. And even if he's not, he'll feel the safety of knowing you're there."

His eyes softened. "Thanks. I'm trying to be patient and let him come to me. But it isn't easy."

"I'm sure it isn't," I said. "But you're one of the most involved parents I've met. Your presence speaks volumes."

Silence settled between us again—thicker, charged with shared respect and something heavier I couldn't identify.

He tilted his head and peeled off his gloves. His thumb grazed my jaw. "You've got a little..." he motioned toward my cheek. "Paint."

I reached for the baby wipes, but he stopped me, pulling one out. Softly cupping my chin like he was cradling something delicate, he paused to study me. The wipe was cool against my skin, but his fingers were warm and firm.

"Rue, you don't have to—"

"Shhh, I want to," he commanded with a quiet power that took me by surprise, arousing the hell out of me.

His strokes were steady and precise, pausing at the curve of my jaw, tracing just under my bottom lip. My breath hitched. He stopped moving, and his brown eyes darted back and forth, never leaving my face.

"There you go," he said after a long pause.

I took a wipe, reached for his temple, brushing gently down his cheek, over the bridge of his nose, then down the edge of his jaw. The air between us tightened as I sipped in shallow breaths.

He closed his eyes, and when I swept just below his bottom lip, he sucked in a sharp breath.

"Rue..."

His eyes slowly opened, assessing me like I was all he wanted.

"Tawni," he said, "I've been wanting to kiss you again for a long time."

My lashes fluttered. "Exactly how long?"

Licking his lips, he whispered, "Since Cherry's Lounge."

"Then what are you waiting for?" I asked, letting my gloves float to the floor.

When our lips met, I didn't expect such softness. His kiss was painfully slow, like he wasn't trying to prove anything and wanted to remember every second. He seemed to have already made up his mind that I was what he wanted. Our kiss deepened gradually, and I leaned into him. We tilted and floated like we were falling backward into a pool of warm water. His arms snaked around my waist, clasping at the small of my back. Mine pushed up his biceps and looped around his neck. We exhaled, then quickly inhaled, sharing a single sweet breath. The moment felt timid. Earned. *Safe.* His lips were familiar, yet compelling enough to keep me yearning for more.

I leaned further into him, and he took the cue, backing me up gently until my spine pressed against the wall. He braced one hand above my head, his palm planted firmly against the drywall, while his other arm remained clamped tight around my waist. His body molded against mine, all heat and tension and longing. My fingers gripped the nape of his neck, drawing out a low hum from his throat.

Each kiss grew hungrier, less measured, like we were both trying to memorize the taste of a moment we didn't want to end. Our breaths turned short and raspy, shared in desperate exhales between kisses. His weight anchored me, his thigh brushing mine, and no matter how hard I fought, my knees threatened to betray me.

Three sharp knocks against the door caused us both to jump.

"Hey, y'all—there are two minutes left in your session, so you may want to start cleaning up," someone called from the other side of the door.

Rue exhaled a groan and dropped his forehead to mine. "Who was that? And why did bruh have to use all that bass in his voice?"

I laughed against his chest, reluctant to pull away. "That might've been the most intense moment I've ever experienced in a plastic poncho."

He chuckled, and I reached up to brush a fleck of coral paint from his earlobe. With a half grin, he said, "Hopefully you managed to stay dry."

I froze, heat rising to my cheeks. The way he said it, playful but low and edged with heaviness, was anything but innocent.

I shot him a look while peeling off the paint-splattered gear and placing it into the labeled basket. "Depends on your definition of dry," I said with a wink. When I glanced over and caught his stunned expression, I smirked. *Serves his ass right.*

Payback's sweet—he wasn't the only one who could play dirty when someone's running on a dry spell.

But as I smoothed out my dress, my fingers trembled slightly. Adrenaline of almost getting caught or an aftershock of our kiss?

We cleaned up in silence, exchanging quiet smiles. His hand found the small of my back, and the twist of my hips said it all. We'd crossed a line, and neither of us wanted to go back.

Chapter 17
Rudolph

I knew today would try me when my work phone buzzed just before sunrise. Yawning, I stretched, then reluctantly pulled it off the charger. When my eyes finally focused, I frowned, cursing under my breath. *Permit delay.* That was the subject line. No good morning, no apology. Just a link to a PDF outlining all of the legal complications and a new round of headaches.

By the time I showered, dressed, and made it to the site, Chase was already forty minutes late. Again. I stood at the edge of the gravel lot, imagining snapping his thick red smoothie straw in half.

"Hey, Rudolph! Sorry, traffic was crazy," he called out, trotting over with his bright eyes and a grin, completely oblivious to the mood.

I didn't respond. At least not with words. Just one glare made him flinch and quicken his pace toward the trailer.

I gave him the benefit of the doubt during week one. And two. But by week five, when the same damn excuses kept popping up like a broken record, that grace had run smooth out.

"Hurry up and clock in, Chase. Then double-check the loadout for Tuesday. I'm not fixing another one of your errors on the delivery sheet."

"Yes, sir."

I winced. Not because of the formality, but because his incompetence was painful. I could literally feel my blood pressure spiking.

Inside the trailer, blueprints were spread out like a jigsaw puzzle mid-solve. Two subcontractors were already bickering over the framing schedule, their voices climbing in volume and tension. My temples throbbed as I massaged the back of my neck, willing the pressure to ease up. Waiting in my inbox were fourteen unread emails from this morning, including one from my supervisor, Glenn. I hovered over it, then clicked off of it. He'd want answers, updates, and solutions. I didn't have any for him right now, so there was no need to expend that mental energy.

I rubbed my palms down the front of my jeans and released a long breath through my nose, jaw tight. I was good at this job because I liked solving problems and being someone others could rely on. I thrived on structure and results. I even appreciated the perks—especially Glenn's flexibility when I needed to be there for Cameron's games, chess tournaments, and school meetings.

But lately, it was all becoming too much. The mounting pressure was a second skin that clung to me no matter how hard I tried to shrug it off. My shoulders stayed locked in place, a constant ache between them from holding up the weight of everyone else's expectations.

I paced the narrow space of the trailer, fingers dragging down the stubble of my beard, trying to think and breathe. I was the glue. The one who showed up, the problem-solver, and the backup plan. But the weight and pressure of the myriad responsibilities were slowly but surely breaking me down. I couldn't help but wonder—who was showing up for me?

* * *

By noon, the crew and staff were all on their lunch breaks. I clutched my phone in one hand and a half-eaten protein bar in the other. My neck was still tight, and my patience was worn thinner than the wood laminate flooring. In the past hour, there'd been a plumbing issue in unit three, a permit delay for unit six, and a supply delivery that was rerouted to the wrong site—over 50 miles away.

I was texting one crew, emailing another, and coordinating a conference call when Glenn strolled in with his usual smug expression, his fresh-pressed polo clinging to his round belly. He looked well-rested, like he'd just walked out of a country club.

His eyes fell on me, and his head tilted back. "Damn, you look like hell, Edwards."

His comment was made in jest, but I wasn't in a joking mood. "Appreciate that, Glenn," I said, looking back at my laptop.

He dropped into the visitor chair and crossed one leg over the other. "Listen. You're a beast. Nobody can ever question that. But I'm gonna need you to start easing up on the team. You're starting to get a rep around here."

I looked at him. "A rep?"

He nodded. "As a hard-ass. A micromanaging ticking time bomb. The guys always feel like they're walking on eggshells around you."

I leaned back in my chair, letting the worn leather creak under the weight of my restraint. I didn't speak right away. I just studied him. Watched how he lounged comfortably with no clue what the daily pressure of my job felt like. No idea what it meant to carry a team that kept dropping the ball or to be the last line of defense when everything hit the fan. He had the nerve to show up with barely a wrinkle in his freshly pressed shirt and tell me to soften up. Like being the nice guy ever kept a project on schedule. My stress level was the only reason this build hadn't gone completely off the rails.

Glenn stuck his hands in the air. "Look, I wouldn't bring this to you if I didn't think it mattered. But I've been hearing things—and I know you're carrying a lot."

Nodding slowly, I asked, "You want me to lead softer? With who, Glenn? The crew that no-shows on site days? The project coordinator who thinks his work schedule's a mere suggestion?"

"I'm just saying—maybe delegate more. Trust the team to deliver. You've trained them well, and they're fully capable."

My brow climbed on its own. *This guy must be kidding.* "I've *been* trusting them. That's why I'm always the one coming in at the crack of dawn, cleaning up everyone's mess."

"I get it. But this can't be sustainable, Rue. Sometimes you have to let them make their own mistakes and learn from them."

"And exactly whose head is on the pike when that happens, Glenn?"

He sighed and leaned against the edge of the drafting table. "Look, I'm not saying let the place burn down. But you're doing damage control before the fire even starts. That's not leadership —that's martyrdom." He waited a beat, eyes steady on mine. "I know you think the whole site would crumble without you, and honestly? Sometimes it does. But you being the only line of defense isn't sustainable. It's not fair to you, and it's not giving your team the chance to step up, either."

I started to respond, but Glenn stood and cut me off. "You

want to build things that last, Edwards? Then stop trying to be the whole damn foundation. Let them take a few hits. If they fail, we'll deal with it. Together. But I need *you* to still be standing by the time this last string of projects is done."

I didn't answer right away. I let my gaze return to the blueprint. At all the lines and numbers and precise angles. At the illusion of control. That's what drew me to this career in the first place. Plans made sense. People sure as hell didn't.

After a moment, I exhaled and said, "You know this isn't just another build for me, right?"

Glenn tilted his head, watching me closely. "Yeah, I know that."

But do you really? "Glenn, this center..." I paused, steepling my hands and resting them beneath my chin, "is for kids like my son whose needs require a different form of learning. So many kids fall through the cracks and don't have enriching afterschool programs or summer camps with leaders who look like them and understand where they come from. This place will be more than brick and drywall. It's a shot for members of our future generation who usually don't get a fair one."

Glenn looked away for a beat, like he was letting the weight of my words settle somewhere real.

"I'll be honest—I hadn't thought about it like that. But you're right. This place does matter differently."

"I know I've been on edge lately," I continued. "And yeah, maybe I'm pushing harder than usual. But it's not pride or control talking. There's a lot at stake for more than just us if we miss more deadlines or get even one more small thing wrong."

Glenn let out a slow breath, then nodded with pursed lips. "Okay, Rue. That's fair. I can respect the hell out of that."

I looked at him, half-expecting a lecture. Instead, he gave me a tired smile. "Then let's make sure it's everything it needs to be—for them and for you. Just promise me you won't grind yourself down to dust in the process."

"I'll try," I said, smiling for the first time in hours. "But I can't make any promises."

He chuckled, then patted the table. "That's all I ask, Edwards. Remember, we're in this together."

He turned and headed out of the trailer, leaving the weight of his words behind.

* * *

By four-thirty, I was alone in the trailer, leaning back in my chair with the blinds half-closed. I knew this wasn't healthy—skipping lunches and pushing myself to the limit each day. The endless drive to stay sharp because the moment I let up, something always fell apart. Still, this project was different. This wasn't just another high-rise, strip mall, or office building. We were standing up a state-of-the-art educational center just east of downtown, in a neighborhood that hadn't seen new development in over a decade. It would offer free after-school programs in coding, digital art, culinary training, music production—all designed for youth who'd been told too often what they *couldn't* do.

I thought about Cameron and how kids like him thrived in a relaxed space where they could explore who they were outside of a school building. A safe space to create, to try and fail, and try again with a dedicated team of professionals to give them individualized guidance. This wasn't just work. This was my offering to my city.

Pressing my fingers into my temples, I inhaled deeply and made a mental note to follow up with the grant partner later this week. We were close—just a few permits away from breaking ground on the multipurpose studio. But getting there felt like running a marathon in concrete shoes.

A text notification yanked me from my thoughts. I picked up my phone.

Tawni: Just confirmed our date for Thursday evening. No need to bring anything. I've got it all covered 😊

I smiled wide, feeling my whole body exhale at once.

Me: Sounds great. I'm looking forward to it.

I set my phone on the desk.

Being with Tawni was perfect. I didn't have to fix anything or anticipate disaster, fearing someone had somehow got it all wrong. She was always present, intentional, and thoughtful. She made sharing space with her feel like a sanctuary.

But she scared the shit out of me, too. I couldn't map out a workflow for love or put developing emotions on a schedule. Navigating the hard moments wasn't something I could cross off my checklist. And part of me—maybe the most honest and exhausted part—wasn't sure I knew how to let someone else show up for me. It felt like almost a lifetime since I'd done that. Still, I wanted to try. Even if it meant loosening my grip, moving forward without having all the answers, and leaning into an unpredictable experience with my full weight.

I double-checked my calendar. Thursday evening was open. And I'd be ready.

Chapter 18
Tawni

I loved lakefront concerts. Tonight, the bass was booming through the sand as the rolling waves kissed the shore in sync with the music. Our voices drifted up like smoke in the summer air as friends passed wine bottles and couples swayed in time to the band's smooth R&B cover of Stevie Wonder's "I Just Called to Say I Love You."

It was a good time, but something kept me from fully sinking into the moment. Rue. His body was stock still, but his mind seemed to be racing at high speed. He was partially present—smiling, laughing at the right times, brushing his fingers against mine each chance he got. But the tension that lined his face was a low hum beneath his calm. It was the same unsettled energy I'd learned to recognize in myself after too many days of pretending to be okay.

I glanced up from my drink and caught him staring at the water instead of the stage. He bobbed his head slightly to show he was listening, but he wasn't as relaxed as he usually was.

He suddenly turned to me and asked in a rough voice, "You

ever wonder who you are when no one needs anything from you?"

His question was painfully direct, catching me off guard. "Sir, we are not emotionally equipped for this at golden hour."

When he didn't even crack a smile, only offering a small shrug, it confirmed something was wrong.

"Nah. Just... curious," he said.

The music faded into background noise as I shifted to face him, tucking my legs beneath me.

"Shit, now that you mention it, I guess I *don't* know who I am when no one needs me," I admitted. "I've spent so long surviving, I forgot I'm allowed to demand more than just peace. Like joy, safety, and the ability to stop thinking everything worth having has to be earned through pain."

He nodded and looked at me for so long, I started to wonder if he'd heard me. I felt naked, almost like he was looking right through me. Rue finally smiled, but it didn't reach his eyes.

"Alright," I said, narrowing mine. "What's really going on?"

"What do you mean?"

"You've been off all evening, like you're not even here. You barely laughed when homeboy tripped over a sandcastle, spilling his cups of beer everywhere."

"That shit *was* funny," Rue smirked, but exhaustion rested in his eyes.

"You don't have to protect everyone else from your bad days by pretending they don't exist."

His eyes cut toward the water again. "Nah, it's nothing."

I leaned in, lowering my voice. "But it's not, though. Look, I'm not asking you to bleed out in front of me. I'm asking you to stop and breathe."

He looked at me again, as if weighing his options. Then he

exhaled a long, weary sound. His shoulders immediately dropped by half an inch.

"It's work," he said finally. "I'm the project manager for the construction of a youth center. Permit delays. An unreliable crew. My boss telling me I need to 'lead softer.' Like it's just that easy."

I nodded, waiting for him to continue.

"This is just another project to them, but not to me. The kids we're building this for deserve it. Each generation deserves more than we had. But every time something slips, I feel like I'm the one failing them." He paused, gaze fixed on the horizon. "I'm tired, Tawn. I'm not burned out... but I can see the smoke from here."

Seeing him like this tugged at something in my chest. I reached over and squeezed his hand.

"I wish I could fix it for you," I said. "But since I can't, I'll sit right here with you for as long as you need."

Rue turned his hand and laced our fingers together.

"This center's going to be exceptional," he said. "It'll have art, media labs, mentoring, real pathways into STEM and entrepreneurship. All free. They're making sure we don't just tell kids to dream—they're giving them something to stand on."

I blinked hard, then shook my head. "You're changing lives for generations to come and still worried you're not doing enough."

"It's taking too long," he said. "These kids deserve to have something real that will last."

"They will, Rue," I affirmed. "And I want in. I want to help."

He looked at me like I'd just spoken in a foreign language. "Yeah?"

"Yeah," I said, nodding. "You'll need someone to interpret for the kids who are hard of hearing, right?"

"Definitely." A bit of the sparkle returned to his eyes, and he threw an arm around me. We snuggled, watching the band for a few minutes.

He leaned in a little. "You wanna get out of here?"

I blinked. "You're not enjoying the show?"

His voice was low. "I'm more interested in getting to know you than listening to a cover band, no matter how good they are."

I nodded. I wanted nothing more than to be alone with him.

We walked back to his car, not saying much. He drove past the miles of parked cars further up the shoreline, pulling into a small turnout where the sand met the rocks and the concert noise had long faded behind us. Night had fallen and the silver moonlight rested on the water, and the only sound was the hush of the waves and the occasional chirping crickets.

We stayed in the car with the engine off and windows down. The warm breeze rustled the hem of my cutoff shirt. Rue sat back in the driver's seat, one hand on the wheel, the other resting on his thigh. He didn't look at me right away, thoughtfully staring out at the beach like he needed a second to collect himself. The feeling was mutual.

When he turned to me, his glistening eyes held curiosity. "What got you into sign language?"

I hesitated, but his insistent silence urged me to speak.

"There was this girl," I said slowly. "Farrah. She moved to Cleveland from San Diego in second grade. Her dad was military, stationed nearby for a few years. She was one of the only Deaf kids in our school, and the system did very little to accommodate her. No interpreter. No real support to help her matriculate."

Rue's brow furrowed, but he didn't interrupt.

"I'd watch her sitting alone at recess, day after day. Most

kids just ignored her. Some were mean. I didn't want to be rude, but something in me just couldn't look away. One day, I sat next to her, and we started drawing cartoon versions of ourselves, animals, and our favorite snacks. We'd take turns, laughing and having a blast."

I smiled faintly at the memory. It was still emblazoned in my mind, resistant to the erosion of time. "Eventually, she started teaching me signs, and I borrowed an ASL dictionary from the library. Once I got better, we created our own little language. We became fast friends. Friendship bracelets, matching backpacks, and bi-weekly sleepovers. She taught me this special sign that we used every time we saw each other: 'forever friends.'"

My fingers quickly danced through the motions, muscle memory guiding them.

"She—" My voice caught, and I swallowed. Rue reached for my hand and squeezed it, like he knew the weight of what was coming.

"One day, I returned to school after spring break vacation, and she was gone. I stared at her empty desk all week." I blinked hard. "I eventually found out that her dad got reassigned overseas without warning. It happened so fast we didn't get to say goodbye. I cried for weeks. I'd never felt that connected to anyone before. Losing Farrah so suddenly made me terrified to ever feel that type of connection again."

Rue's jaw tensed, but he nodded and stayed quiet. He rubbed his thumb over my clenched hands, pulling me into him with his right arm.

"I think that's why I pour so much into my work and volunteering. I got back into ASL because I was pulled toward service. Before the world taught me to shrink myself to fit other people's needs, Farrah made me feel like being myself was enough. I kept searching for that unbridled freedom, knowing it was still in here," I pointed to my chest. "Thinking if I just kept showing up for others the way I did for Farrah... I'd feel honored and respected. I wanted to love freely, without armor, but I was afraid to."

Silence settled between us, heavy and sacred. I never realized how quiet Rue was until now. Not just in the absence of words—but in the way he held space. Present, attentive, and actively listening, not just hearing. He let silence stretch intentionally, like he trusted I'd speak when I was ready. His silence didn't demand anything from me. It just made room, and I was grateful.

I looked up at him, sensing his heart was heavy and he also had something to say. I was still leaning against him, so his posture had shifted slightly. He was relaxed but alert.

Finally, he exhaled slowly. "Tawni..." He shifted closer, one hand still in mine. "You didn't just matter to her at that time. You still do. That kind of love doesn't fade. It planted something deep in you, and I see it every time you show up. For your students, for Cam," his voice caught.

Remembering how hard it was for Rue after his wife died suddenly caused an ache to stir inside of me. Not because he said it—he rarely did—but because I'd seen it.

After Willow passed, he was a walking contradiction: steady and responsible on the outside, but emotionally unmoored just beneath the surface. He wasn't breaking into tears during meetings or lashing out at the school faculty and staff. He wore his pain subtly. I'd spent enough time with kids who carried more than their share to recognize what unspoken grief and trauma looked like.

I remember when Rue and Willow first walked into my classroom for Cameron's open house. I felt pride looking at them, portraying the model couple. She was absolutely beautiful and kind. Rue was standing in the background, jostling

Cameron's hair playfully as Willow took the lead in our conversation. Her guidance on how to connect with Cameron proved how attentive and loving she was with him. When she passed away four months later, I was instantly aware of the void she left in their family. Not just in the way Rue showed up quieter and more withdrawn, but in the way Cameron clung to routines like lifelines—how his light dimmed, how his bright smiles took longer to return.

Rue became a shadow of the man I'd first met. Still present, still trying, but it was easy to tell he was swimming through grief just to make it through each day. That's when I knew they needed more than just a teacher. They needed someone to steady them and stand in the gap for them. So, I became that person. Our 9 a.m. parent meetings were usually after Rue had already held up to four work meetings. He was polite but distracted. Wired too tight and running on fumes. Not just tired—grief had hollowed him. He was fighting to remain standing with the scraps he had left of his emotional capital, trying to pour into a grieving son while having nothing left for himself. But even then, it was obvious how much he loved Cameron.

We spent countless hours together that fall, collaborating on lesson adjustments, talking through behavior plans, constant progress report emails. I pulled strings to get Cameron an expedited evaluation for support services and pointed Rue toward a mentoring program that specialized in helping boys dealing with loss. It felt great to matter in that way, showing up with both hands open, ready to help him build something better. The more we worked together, the more change I saw in him.

So when a single tear rolled down his face while his eyes remained firmly set on mine, I wasn't surprised in the least by his next words. "Tawni. You completely rebuilt me."

Even still, sitting in this quiet car with him now, seeing his handsome face crumple in vulnerability and gratitude. Hearing him say how much I mattered to him and Cam was undoing me in unexpected ways.

I reached over and wiped his tear with the pad of my thumb. His hand met mine, and he mouthed the words, "Thank you."

In the middle of my saying "of course," he leaned over and kissed me. Soft. Deep. Slow. His tongue massaged mine, coaxing a moan from deep within me.

The air between us hummed with deep desire. But this time, it was Rue's acknowledgment that made it much more than physical for me. We'd both been silently carrying our burdens, and now we were finally trusting someone else to hold them, if only just for a moment.

Chapter 19
Tawni

When he broke our kiss, I grabbed his shirt and pulled him right back in. Not releasing my grip, I leaned over the console separating us, palming his head with the other hand. I closed my eyes, feeling his returned passion, matching my rhythm, stroke for stroke. He tasted decadent, like dark honey—warm and slow with rich undertones. Our heads bobbed, turned, and twisted as sweet heat escaped our nostrils. His hands brushed down the length of my arms, slipped past my waist, then reached deep into the seat, cupping my ass. I lifted it, giving him full access to its suppleness. My hips rolled in time with my quickening breath —soft, deliberate, and full of intent.

I kicked off my shoes and slid my legs over the console. Without a word, his hand slipped out of view, and we began slowly sinking backward as I straddled him. Once the seat was fully reclined, I rested my full weight on him. Our faces were mere inches apart, and I studied his eyes. I saw a raging inner storm behind all the calmness he tried to portray. Instead of hunger or bravado, his aching shone through. I saw a man who'd been holding himself together with deadlines, dignity, and duct tape. I realized right then that his silence hadn't been a form of distance, but discipline. Rue had been quiet all night because he was unraveling in real time, and he likely didn't trust himself not to fall apart.

His pupils shimmered, unblinking. I instantly felt his weariness. He'd been so strong, but he also had to be tired of being everyone's anchor. In his fragility and rawness, strength and hope permeated our small space. I felt the silent questions: *Can I freefall right here, right now? And will you catch me if I do?*

That's when I knew this wouldn't be about sex for him. Like me, he was searching for safety, to not have to lead for once. To not have to hold it all together. He needed my softness. My reassurance. He needed stillness. And I would be all of that for him tonight.

In a husky voice I barely recognized, I asked, "Did you put the blanket in your trunk?"

He frowned, nodding.

I grabbed my shoes, then leaned over and pressed the trunk release button before stepping out. He followed me, closing the door and leaning up against it, twirling his key ring on his finger as I rummaged through his things, grabbing a large bag holding everything he'd packed for the concert: two soft blankets, pillows, a bottle of wine, cups, a small Bluetooth speaker, and battery-operated fairy lights. Then I snagged Rue's sweatshirt for good measure. I handed him the bag, then led him by the hand out to the beach.

When my feet hit the sand, the cool grains pressed up between my toes. I took my time, letting the anticipation build with every barefoot step, tugging Rue along behind me. The warm breeze had picked up slightly, brushing my bare arms and teasing the hem of my skirt. But I was warmed from the inside—by him, by the promise of what was unfolding.

I led us down to a small inlet tucked behind a ridge of dune grass, a quiet patch where the moonlight shimmered like silver confetti across the lake's surface. We were completely out of sight and free to savor stolen moments of privacy.

"Here," I said softly, taking the blankets from his arms and spreading them out. "Let's make this our home for a little while."

A small smile graced his lips as we arranged the pillows. The fairy lights provided a warm golden glow in the evening air, transforming the space into a cozy nest. Rue sat down first, stretching out his long legs so I could sit between them. I pulled his hoodie over my head. It swallowed me whole, enveloping me with his signature scent. Then I pressed my back to his chest, poured us each a glass of wine, and handed him one before tapping the Bluetooth speaker beside us.

The first soft chord pierced the night air. Neither of us spoke; we just listened with our eyes fixed on the water. After the last note of the third song faded, Rue tightened his arms around my waist, anchoring himself to me.

"Who is this?" he asked quietly. "I need more."

I hesitated for half a beat. "It's me."

He leaned forward slightly, his chin grazing my shoulder. "Those were your songs? They're incredible."

"Yes. I wrote and recorded them. I've been in the studio for the past few weeks trying to get the sound right. I have a showcase to introduce my EP in six weeks."

He pulled back, and I glanced up at his face. His expression told me everything I needed to know. He loved it. "Damn, you're making major moves."

"I've been sitting on this music for years, not quite ready to release it," I admitted. "But it feels like it's now or never."

Rue cupped my face gently, his voice low and firm. "It's definitely now. You're more than ready. And the world needs to hear you."

His words landed deep, seamlessly slicing through my insecurities. I believed him in that moment.

I nodded. "Thanks, Rue. I receive that."

I felt him release a long exhale, like he'd finally allowed his body and mind to stabilize.

"Feeling better?" I asked, tipping my head back and feeling his jaw rest against my temple.

"I am now."

Setting down my empty glass, I turned slowly in his arms, straddling his hips, my knees sinking into the soft sand below the blanket. I cradled his face in my hands and looked into his warm eyes. They were still somewhat vacant, showcasing the silent pain he tried to keep hidden beneath calm tones and half-smiles.

"Rue..." My thumbs brushed along his cheekbones. "You know you don't have to be strong for me, right?"

"At this point, I don't know how to be anything else," he admitted, his voice cracking.

"With me, you don't need to be anything but present," I whispered. "Let me be strong for you tonight."

He closed his eyes, and I could feel the tension spilling out of him as his body softened. When he lay back, I followed, brushing a kiss against the corner of his mouth, then the edge of his jaw, tasting the salt left behind by a tear. His hands slid to the back of my thighs, gripping them firmly as I settled on top of him.

"Right now, I only see you, Rue. Not the successful project manager. Not the devoted father. Not the habitual fixer. Just you."

His hands cupped my face, his thumbs resting against my temples. "Damn... I didn't realize how much I needed to hear that until now."

I leaned in until our lips brushed. "I mean every word of it."

He pulled my lips into a slow, reverent kiss. I felt every ounce of his gratitude. His large hands slowly wandered over my body, like he didn't want to forget this moment. My body arched in response, longing to feel his skin on mine.

He shifted our bodies, and before I knew it, he was on top of me, his eyes focused on mine like I was the only thing on his mind. He lifted my shirt and planted kisses on my stomach. My back lifted off the blanket, and he slid his hand in the crevice beneath, gripping my waist with his other hand. As his tongue swirled over my exposed skin, I gripped his forearm, relishing the wet trail he left behind. His hand massaged my right breast before he slipped my nipple into his mouth. It was my turn to groan as my head lifted off the blanket, tilting back.

"Rue, that feels so good," I said, cradling his head.

Sucking hungrily, he twisted my left nipple between his fingers until it pebbled.

"Mmm. Right there," I whispered, wrapping my legs around his back.

I instantly felt it—gentle pulsing against my stomach. My hand slipped between us to grip his long, hard thickness. He moaned against my neck before moving on to my left breast. His hands found the crown of my head, then smoothed down over my short curls to the nape of my neck.

"Teach... I love how your hand feels around it," he panted before moaning again.

"Mmm, you do?" I asked, concentrating on the way his mouth tightened with each gentle squeeze.

"Don't do this to me, Tawni. I just can't do this right now," he groaned against my chest. There was a tortured edge to his words.

"Can't do what?" I taunted him, reaching into his pants and sliding my thumb over his sticky tip.

I felt the breeze cooling my skin in the absence of his mouth on my breast. His teeth grazed my shoulder bone as a low growl escaped his lips.

I didn't flinch. "Do it again. Harder."

His teeth sank into the side of my neck, and I closed my eyes, savoring the semi-sweet pain. Warmth stirred between my legs before surging throughout my body.

"Yes, yes," I said, gyrating my hips and lifting them to meet his.

My grip on his dick tightened, and he moaned louder.

"I said I can't do this," he snarled into my hair.

"And I said, can't do what?"

He lifted up and looked at me. "Take things slow. Give you the respect you deserve."

I frowned, searching his eyes. "I'm lost, Rue."

"I want to fuck the shit out of you, Tawni," he barked. "I want to twist and contort your pretty little body in every which way and make you shudder, cumming all over this dick again and again. Right here, right now."

The only sound that could be heard was the wind gushing through my ears and the gentle lapping of the lake's waves. When I could only manage to blink and stare at him in confusion, he continued. "I want to turn you the fuck out. I want you to be my Bad Teacher."

When I finally found my voice, I asked, "Then what are you waiting for?" I lifted my hips and pulled back my skirt, then slid off my panties.

He watched in stunned silence as I tossed them aside. With his mouth slightly open, he reached into his back pocket for his wallet. "So glad I slipped this bad boy in this morning," he grunted, sliding out the foil square.

I snatched it from his hands and commanded, "Ground. Clothes off. Show me those good listening skills."

His eyes widened, only for a second. Then that signature half-grin broke across his face, and he dropped and double-timed it like I'd blown a shrill recess whistle. He peeled off his shirt, kicked off his boat shoes, shimmied out of his cargo shorts, and lay on his back in record time. I started to wonder if he'd ever done this kind of drill before.

Remaining in character, I strolled toward him. "That includes underwear."

His toned thighs and abs flexed as he did a glute bridge, lifting his hips off the ground, pressing through his heels. When he slowly peeled off his boxer briefs, my eyes trailed his movements like a man hungrily eyeing his last meal. But his eyes remained on mine. His grin converted to a smirk, and I caught something flash in his eyes. It was deeper than lust. That smirk held a promise: desire, laced with determination. It was turning me on in the worst way.

Towering over him and planting a foot on either side of his body, I said, "Now class, whenever the flag's at full mast, we must salute it." I slowly sank to my knees, bringing the blanket down with me to cover us.

His eyebrows shot up as he watched me tuck the condom in my bra before easing my mouth over a third of his length. His moans weren't immediate. He made me work for them. But I love a challenge. The quieter he was, the more I worked my hands and mouth, twisting and massaging his generous girth until he couldn't hold in his satisfaction any longer.

"Ungh, sing into the mic, T. Lexx," he said, dragging out his words.

That's Bad Teacher to you. But my mouth was too full to

respond. My head bobbed, moving to a beat only we could hear. He mimicked my head motion as he watched me carefully. Just as his legs began to tighten and shake, I released him from my mouth and handed him the condom.

"Suit up, mister. This is a protected activity."

Ripping open the wrapper, Rue lifted a brow and nodded. "Safety first. Just so you know, I excel at group projects, Teach."

"We'll see about that," I said, descending on his erection with precision.

When I reached the base, we gasped collectively, each immediately breaking character. I couldn't believe how good it was to feel him for the first time. His widened eyes told me he felt the exact same way.

"Good God, Rue," I said, clamping my eyes shut.

His fingers gripped my hips so hard, I knew I'd have striped bruises along them in the morning. I tried to find my rhythm, but he fully consumed me, not leaving much wiggle room to work with. With impatience evident on his face, he lifted his hips to meet mine, slamming into me with just enough force to take my breath away.

I placed my hands on his chest to maintain my balance. "That's good. Really good, babe."

His hips lifted repeatedly, with a perfect pace. His movements were fluid. His strokes were easy and measured. I held my breath every other second as our hips met, savoring the delicious feeling of being filled by him.

"Rue, my goodness," I panted, eagerly riding his wave.

He eased his hold on my waist, letting his hips take the lead and causing us to rise and fall together.

"Oh, yes, Teach. Yes," he moaned.

The wine, the waves, the warmth of him—it blurred into something sacred that I knew we'd both treasure for a long time.

"I needed this," he groaned, his voice almost whining.

I nodded and smiled. "Me too."

In the stillness of that moonlit cove, he made good on his promise. We gave one another exactly what we needed. All night long.

Chapter 20
Rudolph

The afternoon sun was high and arrogant, boldly glinting off Lake Erie with intense rays. I was sweating through my tee before we even got the grill set up. Kenny had already been talking trash about our upcoming basketball game. Marcus had hauled in all of the coolers and, stubbornly refusing help from anyone, tipped over the cooler with his mother's world-famous potato salad. Link had shown up with the corn hole board—the only thing I'd asked him to bring—but forgot the sacks at home.

"Man, I swear I can't rely on y'all for nothing," I grumbled, taking a slow swig from my water bottle.

"Dude, calm down. We know you're still salty we bailed on you for the festival last month," Link said, wincing as he slowly lowered himself into a lawn chair. "And before you ask—yes, it's the same back injury I got from trying to block a dunk at the basketball tournament last week. My knees smooth clocked out on me."

"And you should've clocked out wit 'em," I said, tossing him a water. "And this guy over here didn't even let us know his plans had changed," I said, gesturing toward Kenny. "Just pulled his routine disappearing act."

"I operate on a need-to-know basis," Kenny shrugged from behind the grill. "And y'all nosy asses didn't need to know shit."

Everyone laughed.

Marcus sat on the bench, tossing a football up with one hand. "My reason was valid. Have you seen the pics of Shawna I sent in the group chat? I'm talking hair down her back, waist beads, and a body like you wouldn't believe. You bet your ass I risked it all in that BMV office. Dumped your ass quicker than one of those construction trucks of yours."

I shook my head. "Bro, you met her and canceled on us the same day. Even Sprite wouldn't tell you to obey that type of thirst."

Kenny laughed. "That man got one compliment and offered her his last name."

"Y'all sound real bitter for some single dudes," Marcus said. "And I know you ain't over there laughing, Link. Pulling hamstrings trying to hoop with these college kids. You don't need Bengay—you need a whole 'nother insurance plan."

"Whatever," Link said with a smirk. "What about Kenny? He's so M.I.A., I got his number saved as 'Nah. Prolly not.'"

"Man, Kenny RSVP'd to the baby shower for my niece and then finally showed up at her high school play talmbout, 'My bad, bruh. Y'all still doin' gifts?'" Marcus joked.

We laughed again as Kenny sank down on a bench, shaking his head. He knew once we started going in on him there was no turning back.

"Kenny ignores the announcement and reminder texts in the group chat, then wanna act surprised and finally respond when we post pics like, *'Wait, that was today?'*" I said.

Kenny held up his hand and said, "Can we take a moment

to talk about our boy Rue? Ever since he found his new friend, bruh's been mighty scarce."

"I ain't gon' lie," Marcus said, nudging Rue's shoulder. "You've been different lately. All chocolate and happy, starring in a rom-com like Morris Chestnut. You sure this woman don't oil your scalp and rub away all your worries at night with warm shea butter?"

I let out a slow chuckle.

"Damn," Kenny muttered. "So he's not lying?"

Before I could reply, my phone buzzed in my pocket. I pulled it out and saw Tawni's name. Just seeing her name softened me in places that I didn't know could still be tender. I smiled before I even read the message.

"Y'all talked her right up..."

I scanned the park to get eyes on Cameron. He was sitting on a picnic table by the lake, scrolling on his phone as he chatted with his friend Brent from summer camp. Family field days had been a thing since before Willow passed. At first, we stopped doing them because the weight of her absence was too loud. But after a year, Dorian made the call. He argued that Willow would be pissed if we let her memory make joy feel off-limits. So now we made it a point to gather our families at least once a season. It still felt a little foreign sometimes, but now her absence was a softer presence.

I glanced down at my phone.

Tawni: I still have your shades in my purse. I can swing by the park before I head out with Tiff and Trish.

I stared at the screen, unable to reply. Cam was just a few yards away, oblivious to the slow shift happening in my life. I hadn't told him about Tawni yet. I wanted to, but didn't know how. Or maybe I just wasn't ready to see his face when I said the words out loud. Something about seeing her here would make it all feel real. And real was starting to feel like a risk. Still, I wanted to see her.

I typed back before I could overthink it. *We're at Lakefront Park. Bring them only if you're passing by. Kenny's making his famous ribs. Might even save you a plate.*

She sent back a thumbs-up emoji. I didn't know if she would actually show up, but something about the idea of her here—on my turf, around my people—excited me.

* * *

"Yo, Rue! I think you've got company, man," Link called out about forty minutes later.

I was in the middle of refereeing a tug-of-war standoff between Marcus and Kenny's nieces and nephews when I spotted Tawni stepping out of her silver sedan. She wore a sleeveless yellow sundress that hit her toned calves and flowed in the gentle breeze. Her hair looked freshly done, her soft curls framing her face. The sunlight kissed her moisturized skin.

"Be back a little later. We'll pick this right back up," I told the group, who all nodded and dropped the heavy rope in unison.

Tawni spotted me, waved, and headed my way, holding up my shades. "Looks like you'll need these. It's a beautiful day."

I grinned, jogging over. "Yeah, we ended up with great weather."

When I finally got to her, I didn't reach for the glasses. I brushed her fingers with mine and leaned in close, lips grazing her cheek and whispering near her ear, "Appreciate the delivery. Missed you."

She smiled softly. Her fingers lingered on my forearm. "Missed you, too. Even if it's only been two days."

Looking at her bronze skin and curvy body had me ready to

find a secluded place for us. I wanted to pull her into me and at least kiss her the way I had just a couple of nights before, but Cameron was too close. Instead, I slid my hand discreetly down her back and gave the curve of her waist a quick, gentle squeeze.

Her eyes fluttered, and she gazed up at me with expectant eyes as she acknowledged the heat simmering between us. Her longing expression sent chills through me. Then she stepped back with a knowing smile, sensing my caution. "The girls and I are headed to lunch at a spot nearby. Figured I'd drop these off on the way."

"Mm-hmm," I murmured absentmindedly, my eyes traveling over the slopes of her curves with slow appreciation.

"This all looks..." she said, scanning the array of obstacle courses, sports equipment, and a table full of trophies, "more involved than I expected."

"Yeah, I kinda undersold it. We go all out."

When I looked up, her girls had materialized on either side of her like Kelly and Michelle.

"Ohhh," the shorter one said, gesturing toward the guys who were all camped out at the pavilion. "Rue, this the crew?"

The taller one chuckled at her friend's rhyme.

Tawni turned to slowly face her friends, eyes wide. "Tiff, I thought we agreed y'all would stay in the car."

Tiff shrugged. "Girl, are you crazy? We're in the middle of a heat wave. Also..." she wiggled her brows. "We just had to officially meet our new favorite construction man."

I extended a hand to her. "It's a pleasure to meet you, Tiffanie. I'm Rue."

She placed her hand in mine, her firm grip taking me by surprise. "Oh, Tiff's fine. And the pleasure's all mine, Rudolph."

"Rue's fine."

After shaking Tawni's hand, I looked over my shoulder and noticed my friends were watching.

Link, ever the showoff, gave them a politician's wave.

I chuckled. "Since you're all here, ladies, would you like to meet the fellas? We have plenty of food."

Tawni rolled her eyes, but a reluctant smile tugged at her lips. "Ten minutes."

An hour later, her shoes were in the grass, and she was playing tug-of-war, soaking wet and laughing like she was having the time of her life. Cam had managed to convince Tawni to be his partner for the water balloon toss, and she'd been a good sport despite losing in the first round. Trish was grilling Kenny for his ribs recipe while Tiff showed Link some of her custom candles on IG.

From my seat by the grill, I watched Tawni interact with my son. She moved easily, laughed heartily, and encouraged Cameron with a familiarity that was amazing to witness. She wasn't just stunning—she was *good*. Solid. But I'd be lying if I didn't admit that their ease scared the hell out of me. Nothing about what we were doing felt casual anymore. We were past the phase of being able to cut ties and walk away from this easily. Real feelings were starting to get involved. Feelings I hadn't experienced in a long time.

I was covering the food with foil when I heard Cameron burst into that high-pitched laugh—the kind I'd only ever heard with me and his mother. His head was thrown back, and his eyes were closed. He was so carefree. So comfortable. My chest pulled tight, and before I realized it, I was grinding my teeth.

Then a voice behind me called, "Hey, brother. Didn't expect to make it today."

I turned and saw Dorian walking up, wearing shades with his hands deep in the pockets of his shorts. My heart dropped before I could register why. Damn.

He nodded toward the group. "What's up, fellas?"

They all stood to give him dap.

He glanced at Tiff and Trish, then tilted his head toward the lake. "That her?"

"Yeah," I said.

He frowned slightly, but I couldn't read his eyes behind his sunglasses. "Yeah, I had a feeling about her."

After a few moments of silence, he said, "I'm already missing Cam, and it's only been a couple of days."

I nodded, my eyes trained on Tawni and Cameron, now high-fiving after completing a successful balloon toss.

"You good, man?" Dorian asked.

I didn't answer right away. "Yeah," I finally said. "You want a beer?"

Under the weight of his careful gaze, I moved to the cooler, retrieved the beverage, and twisted off the cap before handing it to him.

Dorian took a seat on the nearest bench, and I joined him a few seconds later. "Listen, I hadn't originally planned for Tawni to come through today. It just happened."

Dorian clapped a hand on my shoulder. "Is that what all this nervous energy's about? Brother, relax. Look, man... you gave my sister everything. Time. Patience. Loyalty. For years. And you stayed faithful to her, even after she was gone. Hell, I'm relieved to see Tawni here. I was starting to wonder if you'd ever try dating again."

I turned to face him. "You're really okay with this?"

"Are you for real? I'm more than okay with it. Willow would want you to be happy. She'd *demand* that shit. You think she'd want you to raise Cam on your own forever?"

I wrung my hands, looking down at the sand and grass below my sneakers. "No, I didn't think that at all. I just didn't know if this was all too soon."

Dorian's hand landed on my right shoulder. "Rue. It's been over *three years*. And since you've been with her... you're different, brother."

I didn't have words for him at the moment, but I knew he was right. Tawni was her own sun with her own orbit. I was glad that Dorian could see that.

"I haven't even told Cam about us yet," I admitted. "I don't want to confuse him."

"That's understandable," Dorian said, nodding. "But my only advice on that is don't wait too long. We had several heart-to-hearts during our time together. He's growing into quite a young man, and he can handle a lot more than you think."

I frowned, hot tears pricking the backs of my eyes. I blinked them back, tapping my shoe against the ground.

"He deserves honesty," Dorian continued. "And so does she."

Just then, I spotted my sister, Chandler, heading toward us accompanied by my parents. Chandler's sundress caught the breeze as she waved with her free hand, the other wrapped around Ma's arm. Pops strolled a few steps behind them like he had all the time in the world, nodding and grinning at people at the neighboring pavilion.

I looked over at Tawni, who had also noticed them. She straightened a little, her body shifting like she wasn't sure whether to come over or hang back.

I waved her over, and when she approached, I caught her hand. "Come on," I said. "I want them to meet you."

Her eyes flickered to mine. "Are you sure?"

"Absolutely." I gave her hand a squeeze.

"Hey, y'all—this is Tawni," I said once they reached us. "She's been a huge support system for Cam and me—especially when we were figuring out all the stuff with his IEP. She didn't just help him—she helped *me*."

Ma smiled, reaching out to pat her hand. "I'm Gloria. Thank you, Tawni. That IEP made a huge difference in Cam's learning experience."

Pops nodded, reaching out to shake her hand. "Rudolph Sr. Nice to meet you, young lady. We appreciate everything you've done for Rue and Cam."

Chandler stepped forward and wrapped Tawni in a hug. "Girl, I already love you," she said. "You got my nephew thriving and my brother using his words."

We all laughed, even Cam, who gave me a thumbs-up before going back to launching water balloons with Brent.

Tawni blended in effortlessly. She and Chandler fell into laughter and conversation like they'd known each other for years. I stood back, taking it all in—my people, my son, and this woman who kept showing up in extraordinary ways.

"Hey," I said to Chandler when we were both near the cooler. "Where's your dude?"

She opened a pop and shrugged. "Work. He said he had a last-minute call-in and had to make it up to me."

I didn't say anything right away. Just nodded and grabbed a beer. But in my head, I clocked it. First church. Now this. *Strike two, my guy.* But Chandler was grown. She'd ask for my thoughts when she was ready.

I turned back toward the grill, just in time to hear Pops tell Tawni, "See? You fit in just fine. Might as well go ahead and grab another plate because I know those Philly cheese bratwursts are calling your name."

She laughed, throwing a glance over her shoulder at me, and I swear my heart started beating triple time.

* * *

Later, when the crowd started thinning out, Tawni was still out playing with the kids. She'd spent most of her time with Cameron, talking with him, laughing, and asking questions like she was still responsible for the welfare of that little boy in him. She'd also made the rounds sitting with the fellas, humoring Marcus's dad jokes—although he didn't have children yet—and dodging Kenny's unsolicited life advice. She fit in like she belonged, and I wasn't sure what to do with that feeling.

I was sitting off to the side, drowning out the noise to make room for my thoughts when she appeared at my side.

"Hey you. Where're Trish and Tiff?" she asked.

"They're in your car," I said. "Marcus offered them to-go plates, and that was all it took. They left out singing H-O-T-T-O-G-O, whatever that means."

She turned just in time to catch Marcus in some wild arm choreography, then laughed, seeming to catch on to some kind of inside joke that no one bothered to fill me in on. I figured their shared moment was probably sponsored by Marcus's close relationship with his three tween nieces.

"Let me walk you over," I said, sticking out my arm.

She slid her hand through, gently squeezing my bicep. "Thanks for letting us crash your party."

"It was nice having you here. You're still so good with Cam."

Her eyes softened. "He's always been a cool kid. He's got your eyebrows, though. How unfortunate."

"Wow. Insulting something I can't change about myself. Don't they call that bullying in your line of work?"

She slowed her pace and laughed like she didn't want our moment to end, then grew quiet. "Seeing you like this... with your people and your son. It reminds me why I enjoy spending time with you. I see where Cam gets his coolness from."

We reached her car, and something settled and stirred in

me at once. I stepped in closer, close enough to feel her breath on my neck. "Thanks, Teach. You're pretty damn cool yourself."

I leaned down and finally kissed her, grateful for the privacy of the evening shadows.

She leaned in, pressing her hand to my chest like she could feel my restraint unraveling. When we pulled apart, her eyes searched mine, glossy and dangerous.

"My house in an hour," she said, voice low and promising. "Nightcap."

I brushed her jaw with the back of my fingers. "My parents are taking Cameron to stay the night at Brent's, so you can bet on that."

"I knew you'd make that happen," she said, winking at me.

I opened her door and dipped my head inside. "Nice to meet you, ladies."

Tiff and Trish gave awkward waves, pretending they hadn't just watched us tonguing each other down.

I rapped on the roof of her car twice. "Text me when you get home."

She nodded, but her eyes lingered for a moment before she gave a finger wave and pulled off.

She was only supposed to swing by for a second. But meeting each other's closest friends had quickly changed the game for us. Watching her laugh with my family and seeing Cam light up with her back in his life—I knew this wasn't just a summertime fling. She was already part of the story.

Chapter 21
Rudolph

We'd been sitting on the second floor of the library, going at it for hours. The table held every manual, workbook, and city ordinance binder we could find. Tawni was on her laptop, frowning thoughtfully while chewing on the tip of her fingernail.

After pretending to read the same paragraph in a funding guide for at least twenty minutes, I decided to take a break. Watching her sitting there, mumbling to herself and tapping her pen against her cheek while wearing those red-framed glasses was doing things to me. I couldn't concentrate on anything else.

"You've been pretending to read that page forever," she said without looking up from her screen.

"I got distracted."

Giving me side-eye, she asked, "By what?"

I leaned in close enough to smell the mocha latte on her breath, hoping to provide a distraction of my own. "By you."

She tried to hide it, but I caught the corners of her mouth curling. "Ugh, you're so annoying."

"And yet, here I am, co-writing this grant proposal with you in a freezing cold library. I knew this would be a thankless job."

She muttered something under her breath that I couldn't quite hear, but I caught her smile. I rubbed her thigh, then began slowly massaging it. Despite the blasting AC, it was soft and warm.

"Stop it, boy," she said, trying to shift away from me. "Let's talk timelines. I've got the three community partners listed. Now I need a rollout plan for the workshops."

I nodded, forcing myself to focus. "I suggest you stagger them: elementary, middle, high school. You can start with exposure—career days, job shadowing. Then move into training programs, internships, HBCU tours. With your focus on inclusivity, interpreters, transportation, and adaptive equipment, we're checking all the boxes."

She looked at me, and it took me a moment to figure out what she was thinking. Then I saw the light bulb go off. "Yes," she said. "That's exactly what I want this to be. The program will start by filling skills gaps, then continue evolving as the students progress through them. I want to establish a defined path from elementary school to the workforce."

Her voice was assertive in a way that helped me see it. I immediately believed in her vision and her ability to develop it. She'd had her aha moment, and our work was pretty much done. After watching her for a few more moments, I sidetracked the conversation. "How do you feel about us?"

She didn't pretend not to get it, which was exactly what I liked about Tawni. She didn't play games.

"I feel good. But I do have some concerns at times that we're moving too quickly."

It was like she was speaking my fears out loud. I glanced down at my hands, then back at her. "The thing about knowing someone before you start dating is sometimes you fall quicker than you normally would have. I know neither of us is there yet, but I'd be lying if I said I wasn't close."

Her hand landed in my lap. "I think we'd both be."

My throat tightened as I looked at her. Her eyes were shining with unshed tears, making me wonder what had caused them. She gave my fingers a squeeze, and I squeezed hers back. This woman was doing things to me I didn't expect or understand.

I cleared my throat and smiled. "We should probably call this a wrap. Because the way you're looking in those glasses and cutoff shorts got me ready to draft some vows instead of a budget."

She cackled, then immediately waved apologetically when a librarian shot us a sharp look. "Stay focused," she whispered, still laughing. "This grant is literally securing my second job."

I leaned back and folded my arms, smirking. "Exactly. You need to feed me after this. I've clocked about three hours of unpaid work so far while struggling to behave myself around all these librarians."

She batted her eyes, leaning in as I placed my hand on the small of her back. "That's fair. As long as you can provide the dessert."

"Say less," I said, stacking up the books in haste and carrying them, ten at a time, back to the closest library cart.

* * *

The evening lake air had cooled drastically as the sun tucked behind the clouds, winding down from the day. Cameron and I had enjoyed jet skiing across the lake for the past hour. After docking them, we ditched our life vests and wet shoes to walk the shoreline barefoot while we dried off. The water lapped at our feet as they sank into the sand, and a few seagulls circled in the distance, their shrill calls echoing in the air.

"You have fun?" I asked.

"Yeah. We haven't done that in a while."

"So how was your sleepover at Brent's?"

"He's new to the neighborhood, and there was a block party on his street last night," he said between bites of the loaded nachos we'd picked up at a food truck. "I saw a lot of kids from school. A girl I didn't recognize was there. She kept riding her bike up and down the block, pretending she didn't see us."

I smirked. "How do you know she was pretending?"

He grinned. "I mean, she was riding all slow with a group of girls. But she eventually glanced at me like three or four times."

I cocked my head and looked at him walking with his chest poked out. "Sounds like you might be as irresistible as you think you are."

Which means he was watching her like a hawk the entire time. I sighed and shook my head. I wasn't ready for this stage—where the trouble begins.

He shrugged, trying to play it off, but his smile gave him away. "She finally stopped to talk to us. She's here visiting her cousin for the summer. I thought about asking for her number. You know. Rizz her up a little bit for a quick summer romance."

"With that 'ol Edwards charm?"

When nothing but silence followed, I glanced over at him just in time to catch an exaggerated eye roll.

"What?"

"Dad, we both know you don't have an ounce of game anymore. It's all dried up like this chip," he said, holding up a nacho before dramatically crunching into it.

I stole one and popped it in my mouth before mumbling, "Boy, I've lost more game than you'll ever have."

Cameron laughed, waving his hand dismissively. "Okay. You got it, Dad."

We walked a few steps in comfortable silence, taking in the beautiful view before us. I noticed his shoulders had broadened over the past year, and his voice was starting to catch more often. I was watching my boy turn into a young man in real time, and seeing him walk shirtless right beside me, almost hitting my shoulder, let me know just how fast it was all moving.

"So," I started casually, keeping my tone light, "how was it seeing Ms. Alexander at the cookout the other day?"

He didn't even blink. "It was cool; she's always been chill."

I nodded, but I could feel my pulse spike a little. "You sure?"

Cameron kicked at a pebble with his heel. "Dad. You were looking at her like she was one of your prized cigars."

I laughed, caught off guard. "What? I—nah, that's not—"

When he cut me off with a side-eye, I relented. He continued, "It's fine. I'm not mad at it. She's nice. Funny. And she smells really good."

I stopped walking. "That's true, but why do *you* know that?"

He laughed even harder. "Half the boys in my class had a crush on her in third grade. When she visited the middle school last year, she was teaching us how to sign. One kid kept acting like he didn't get it just so he could stare at her longer."

I shook my head, remembering my pre-teen years. "Were you ever crushing on her?"

"Nah, I wasn't really into girls until this year. But," he said, tossing his empty nacho tray into a nearby bin, "you didn't do too bad for yourself in selecting a 'friend.'" He dramatized his air quotes.

We shared a chuckle. A little part of me knew that we weren't fooling Cameron.

"Look, Cam, I want you to know that neither of us expected this to happen," I said. "But I do like Ms. Alexander a lot. The reason you haven't really seen me dating is... I didn't want to get serious with anyone who didn't understand how important you are to me."

He was quiet for a beat, then said, "Yeah, I could tell. Ms. Alexander has always talked to me like I'm a whole person. Even now, she doesn't just see me as your kid."

I swallowed hard. "You *are* a whole person."

"I know," he said, pulling on his tee. "But you'd be surprised how many adults only treat us like who we belong to or what we've done in the past. Like they can't see past those things. Or maybe they're not interested in getting to know who we are. I'm just glad that's not the case with you or her."

I nodded, maintaining my cool on the outside while his quiet truth brought an air of disappointment that hit me square in the chest. Cameron had always been an internal thinker and feeler and rarely shared things like this. So I was learning that everything he said didn't require a response. It was more important to just let him get his thoughts out so he could figure out how he was feeling about these things. We walked for a few more minutes in thoughtful silence before I reached over to ruffle his damp twists. He dodged my touch, pretending to be embarrassed since we were in public.

"But really, do you ever feel weird about me dating again?" I asked. I needed to hear it from him.

He glanced at me, then back at the lake. "I used to. But not with her. It's just different. She's always felt... I don't know... safe. And I like seeing you happy. You've been laughing much more since she's been in your life. And you don't look so tired."

My lips moved, but I couldn't find any words for a moment.

Nodding slowly, I let his words sink in as we kept walking. No matter how I tried to keep it from him, he still noticed how exhausted I was. I didn't know how to feel about that. I could only hope that he saw how important it was to me that I provided for him while also demonstrating the value of hard work. I was hard on him, but I wanted him to see that I also walked the walk.

"But uh, Dad?"

"Yeah?"

Cameron shoved his hands in his trunk pockets. "She got a niece or sumthin'?"

I paused, caught off guard for the second time that evening. When I caught the glint of humor in my son's eyes, I laughed so loud it scared off an entire flock of seagulls.

Chapter 22
Tawni

I didn't realize how tense I was until I finally eased into my car, gratefully letting the door slam behind me. The quiet was thick, almost suffocating. I rested my forehead on the steering wheel and released a long, shaky breath.

I had to fight back tears in the hospital room located in the pediatric wing, knowing I couldn't allow emotion to distract or confuse my clients. But now, my chest throbbed with the ache of holding it all in.

The patient—a little girl named Rozlyn—couldn't have been older than seven. Big brown eyes. Chunky cheeks. A custom Disney princess hospital gown that showed she was loved and cared for. Her hearing had faded fast, her mother explained. An autoimmune disorder had turned their whole world upside down. Rozlyn's sense of hearing was diminishing quickly. One day she was laughing gleefully at Cocomelon jingles, and now she flinched when too many people talked at once and cried when she couldn't make out her mom's voice. She had recently stopped talking altogether.

It was supposed to be a simple visit—a follow-up appointment and a few recommendations for therapeutic toys and visual tools. But when I walked in, Rozlyn was wailing on the exam table, and her mom was frozen, tears streaming silently down her face.

"She keeps gesturing for me to pick her up, but I can't understand what she's saying," the mother had said, almost choking on her words. "She keeps signing something, but it isn't what the nurses taught her. I—I don't know what it means."

My mentor hadn't made it yet due to an accident on I-90. So it was just me—my first solo medical event unchaperoned. I eased into the room, glancing at a note on the dry-erase board. Rozlyn knew her ASL alphabet, and there was a list of terms she'd learned. Thankful for the attending nurse's breadcrumb, I crouched down low and caught Rozlyn's terrified gaze. She looked panicked, desperate. Her head was buried in her mother's arms. I signed slowly and clearly: *It's okay. I'm here to help. My name is Tawni.*

Rozlyn's crying slowed to hiccups. Her eyes closed for a moment in an exhausted haze. Then she opened them again. I glanced at her fingers, which remained clenched into tight little fists. However, her eyes, full of tears, were fixed on me. I read the confusion in her eyes. *Can I trust you?* My heart clenched as I imagined all of the detrimental changes she'd recently endured, but I had to remain focused.

I pointed at her striped stuffed elephant, trapped in her firm grip. *Who is this?* I signed, my eyes wide with wonder.

After a few moments of watching me closely, Rozlyn released the elephant from her grasp and offered him to me.

"That's her favorite toy. I had him custom made for her as soon as I found out I was pregnant. His name is Tusky," her mother said, her hand hovering around her mouth.

I nodded at mom. Then my mouth dropped open, and I gestured toward my chest, mouthing the question, *For me?*

Rozlyn released a warm giggle, her eyes crinkling while catching the overhead light. She nodded and shoved the elephant into my waiting arms. I gave the plush toy a big, dramatic hug, rocking him from side to side. Then I held him at arm's length and examined him. I looked back at Rozlyn and signed the words: *Hurt? Where?*

Gently placing the toy back into her arms, I widened my eyes and shrugged my shoulders. With a tiny finger, Rozlyn pointed to the elephant's big round tummy, then to her own tummy. Then she signed something back—sloppy, but familiar. *Hurt. Tummy.*

Her mom gasped, finally recognizing the signs now that some of the tension had eased. "Did she say her stomach hurts?"

I nodded.

"You doing okay in here, Rozlyn?" the nurse signed as she walked in.

I responded, "She's signing about pain in her stomach."

The nurse washed her hands, then began gently pressing around Rozlyn's abdomen. The little girl's eyes widened in fear, but I stayed in view, pointing to Tusky and gesturing for Rozlyn to point to exactly where it hurt. After a few seconds, Rozlyn let out a little toot. After shock registered on her face, her chubby cheeks rose, and she broke into a fit of uncontrollable giggles.

"Toot, toot," she screamed in a high pitch so loud it made us all jump.

Calm washed over Rozlyn's nurse's face. Her mother joined her daughter in giggles. I smiled.

Her mother thanked me repeatedly. When I left a half hour later, after watching them smiling with their arms wrapped around each other, the heaviness left with me. I felt depleted. I couldn't get Rozlyn's echoing sobs out of my head. I was composed, clear-headed, confident, and comforting—all critical components of a first-time interpreter. And I was proud of that.

But I also felt hollowed out. Yes, we'd found a solution, but I hated that Rozlyn had to experience losing her hearing in the first place. When I finally lifted my head and stared out the windshield, I noticed the sky had turned dusky orange. The color made everything feel heavier. I needed to talk to someone who wouldn't ask a thousand questions—a person I could trust who wouldn't need a full debrief of what had just happened to understand how I felt.

For the very first time, I scrolled right past Tiff, Trish, and my mother's numbers in my call log. When I found Rue's name, I tapped call. He picked up on the second ring.

"Hey." His voice was warm and low, coating my ears in velvet. "I wasn't expecting to hear from you this early. Everything good?"

I replied in my mind. But my lips wouldn't move. My voice was held captive by a sob I refused to release.

"Tawn? You there? What's going on?"

I shook my head, knowing he couldn't see me. When I finally managed to swallow, I whispered, "Yeah, I'm okay. It's just been... a day."

He was quiet for a beat, probably expecting more from me, but I had nothing more to give.

He finally said, "I'm sorry, babe. You wanna talk about it?"

It was my turn to hesitate. As much as I wanted to unload on him, I wasn't sure how much to share. Rue was already dealing with his own issues with work. But I thought about our handshake at the arboretum—how we promised to be each other's person. I took a shaky breath, then exhaled.

"I unexpectedly had my first solo assignment at a hospital today. The attending nurse had to leave early, and we were called in at the last moment. My colleague, Hannah, was caught in traffic, and the situation was escalating quickly. The patient was a little girl who had just lost most of her hearing. She and her mom were both overwhelmed because the mom didn't know how to communicate with her daughter. She was only seven—in pain, scared—and I just..." I swallowed hard. "Of course, I kept it together in the moment, but now that I've let myself start to process it all, I feel like my mind is all jumbled."

Rue didn't rush to speak, and I was grateful to have those few moments to take a few deep breaths. When I was done, I realized he was taking them right along with me. His voice was gentle when he said, "It sounds like you carried a lot today."

"It didn't feel like it in the moment. I just did what needed to be done. I didn't expect it to hit me like this," I admitted. "In training, they tell you to stay neutral. To be the bridge, not the story..."

"That makes sense."

"Well, I *was* the damn bridge. I was holding everyone up. But I still feel every tire track now that it's all over. Yes, I helped solve a minor issue, but that little girl is still in there suffering."

He let out a soft breath, signaling that he was sitting with my words. "Tawn... you weren't just a liaison. You were their lifeline. Her mother needed hope, and that little girl needed a sense of calm. They got that because of you."

My eyes stung again. I turned my face toward the window, watching the shadows stretch across the parking lot.

"But also," he added gently, "you're not expected to have the cure. You're there to ease the tension. To make sure people can understand each other when it matters most. That's powerful. Fluency, clarity, presence—that's what you offer. That's the gift you give."

The tears I'd been keeping at bay finally slipped free.

"I just wanted her to feel safe," I whispered.

"And she did," he said. "Because you showed up."

I nodded, sucking in a shaky breath. That was the thing with Rue—he never rushed to fix my pain, but he also never let me carry it alone. "How do you do it? How do you pour into others like this and still have something left?"

He was quiet again, and then said, "Sometimes I don't. But I try to give myself room for restoration after—space to refill. That's what I'm learning—about fatherhood, about management—I don't have to always have it all together. I just do my best not to let the weight harden me."

His words nestled into my chest, bringing comfort, weight, and truth.

"I wish you were here," I said softly, surprising myself.

Rue didn't miss a beat. "Me too."

Quiet hung between us for a few seconds.

"Can I see you tonight?" he asked.

My heart tugged toward those words I'd been waiting to hear. I hadn't planned on it. But I didn't want to be alone tonight.

"I'd love that," I whispered.

"Okay. I'll come to you."

"I'll stop for Chinese. Bring sparkling wine."

"You got it, Teach."

* * *

I gripped my ceramic mug at a café near my home, trying to still my jumping leg under the table. I was working off of less than four hours of sleep and needed every bit of the caffeine in my morning espresso. After Rue left, I'd tossed and turned all night, still haunted by Rozlyn's cries.

Ms. Karr walked up to my table, bringing a sweet citrusy

scent with her. She gave me a brief hug before sliding into the seat across from me. After taking one look at me, she raised an eyebrow.

She signed, "You look beautiful, but also like someone in the throes of some serious soul-searching."

I let out a low laugh, then signed back, "If that's your clinical term for crying in a parked car until your stereo becomes your therapist, I'd say you're spot on."

She smiled, but her eyes held empathy as her hands moved fluidly. "I got your text, but figured we should meet in person. Tell me what happened."

I exhaled and told her everything—from the moment I stepped into Rozlyn's hospital room to the second I collapsed behind the wheel of my car. I let her know how badly I wanted to both fall apart and be invisible at the same time.

Ms. Karr leaned in with her hands folded in front of her. Just her presence and attention helped calm me.

"Pediatrics will pull at you like that," she signed. "Especially when the interpreter is the calm in the midst of the storm. You did everything right. But just because you're steady doesn't mean it won't still shake you."

"I wasn't ready for how hollow I felt afterward," I admitted, enunciating so she could lip-read. "I was proud of myself in the moment, but the second I sat down, I felt like my energy had been scooped out by the bucketful."

Her eyes were trained on me, and although I initially intended to leave it at that, something made me continue. "Something about seeing that little girl in that huge hospital bed, afraid and struggling to connect with her own mother, took me back to my childhood. To a person very dear to me."

Ms. Karr tilted her head. "Sounds like you saw more than just a patient, sweetheart. You want to tell me about this person?"

I hesitated. I knew Ms. Karr could help me, but I wasn't sure I had the energy to discuss it at that moment.

"No pressure to share at all. But I've learned that saying it out loud sometimes makes the weight easier to carry."

When I looked up and took in her concerned expression, I found the strength to open up. I told her about Farrah. "When she began teaching me signs, I'd found a hidden passageway into her world, and it made me feel useful."

My fingers absently signed *forever friends*—and I caught the glimmer in Ms. Karr's eyes.

"She gave me a new language, and I gave her loyal friendship. That exchange shaped everything. It made me want to show up for other kids in the ways trusted adults couldn't show up for Farrah. It made me want to be the bridge—not just a helpless witness."

I took a sip of my lukewarm coffee. "That's what was so hard about seeing Rozlyn in that hospital bed. I recognized the fear in her eyes, and I hated to think about the journey ahead for both of them. That there's nothing significant I can do to help them."

I glanced at Ms. Karr. "Hospitals are about urgent care. But schools and programs provide possibilities. I don't want to only show up when there are emergencies. I want to be there before the cracks turn into breaks. That's where I belong. Not just interpreting words, but giving kids back their voice."

"Yes! That feeling is your compass," Ms. Karr signed excitedly. "It's not pointing you away from interpreting altogether, just maybe away from this particular lane. There's a difference between being capable and being called."

It was my turn to nod in silence.

"You're allowed to opt out of this kind of work—or at least not consider it long-term. It takes a specific kind of stamina to walk into fresh trauma every day and still have something left for yourself." Her hands paused mid-air, then her face softened. "What you did yesterday was heroic. Truly. But if it's draining you dry, that doesn't mean you're incapable. It means you're aware enough to notice what your spirit has the capacity to carry."

Conflicted and confused, I stared into my cup, watching the last swirls of crema dissipate.

She waited until I looked back up, then added, "You have such a deep love for children, Tawni. That's always been evident. But maybe that love runs too deep to witness them in pain. You're an extraordinary educator—nurturing, inspiring. You're wired to help them bloom, not just survive. And that's okay."

I nodded, fighting back tears. Ms. Karr had grown to know me so well, and her words tapped into a purpose that I hadn't yet identified. I couldn't ignore how critical this moment was, even though it was laced in pain.

"You mentioned applying for a youth grant when we last talked," she said. "How's that going?"

I was grateful for the shift, even though my chest was still tight with unsettled feelings. "It's for a youth center that my colleague, Rue, is building—they're securing programming for next year. He and I have been working on a proposal for a career-readiness program: skill-building, mentorship, and career guidance. My sector would focus on assisting Deaf and hard-of-hearing teens."

Watching her face light up brought me joy. I smiled for the first time that day. "Yes! That's exactly what I hoped you'd say. I just came from a district advisory meeting this morning, and they're actively looking to fund programs like this, especially those focused on inclusion. Since your grant proposal is already done, you'd be walking in with exactly what they've been asking for."

My eyes widened. "What? That's great news. How much is the grant for?"

"It depends on the structure of your proposed program," she said, flipping to the second page of her notebook. "But most youth-centered career readiness programs like this pull from multiple sources. There's a $50,000 startup grant from the county for curriculum and staffing, another $25,000 earmarked for accessibility resources—which would partially cover your salary as a certified interpreter—and then multiple smaller grants for materials, transportation, and enrichment activities. If the proposal's solid, you could lock in $150K or more."

Her response wasn't what I expected. Securing grants totaling $150,000 would solidify my position as Career Pathways Educational Director and fund the resources outlined in our proposal for at least the first two years.

"And I've heard from a few parents lately—Deaf teens have been asking about future options, but there aren't enough support systems or ASL-fluent mentors in place to bridge that gap."

My mental fog finally lifted. "Ms. Karr, this feels right. Like I'd be helping build something that will make an impact. One that I'm more than qualified to provide."

Her smile radiated through me. "Exactly. You're not only a bridge, Tawni. You're a builder." She reached for my hand and squeezed it. "Give yourself permission to go where your gifts are most needed. Because the Deaf community needs more advocates like you."

Chapter 23
Tawni

A few days later, after finishing an hour-long morning hike in the Metroparks with Jaclyn I rushed home to shower, change, and meet up with Rue. We'd spent hours finalizing the youth center's grant proposal and discussing logistics for the after-school enrichment programs.

I was curled up on Rue's couch while scanning the final edits. We'd just finished lunch when Rue came over with a fresh cup of tea. Instead of returning to the kitchen, he leaned in and kissed my forehead. When I smiled, he moved on to my cheek. Then my neck.

Soon, the laptop slid from my lap to the couch cushion as I prepared for his body to join mine.

"You know," I murmured as his lips found the side of my neck, "if every time we work on this final draft, I have to fight off your horny self, it's never going to get finished."

Rue smirked against my skin. "It's three-quarters of the way done. I think we've earned a break."

The desire in his eyes burned with intensity. I straddled him, and we kissed like neither of us had anything else to do. I was thrilled to let myself partake and be taken. Just as I was about to slip my bra out of my shirt sleeve, I heard a car door slam in the driveway.

Rue froze. One hand was still gripping my waist, the other cradling the back of my neck. His breath stalled. "Shit."

My heartbeat stuttered as I sat up. "What was that?"

He exhaled sharply, shifting me gently to the side. "I'm pretty sure that's Cameron."

"How?"

"He takes a carpool to chess club, but he's not supposed to be back for—" he glanced down at his watch. "—for another hour." He was already on his feet, smoothing his shirt. "He doesn't have his key today. I need to get the door for him."

I grabbed the laptop, my face flushed with a heat that no longer had anything to do with desire.

Cameron knocked on the door. His tone was casual as he called out, "Dad?"

Rue shot me a look, and I nodded before he opened the door.

I heard Cameron's cheerful voice as the door opened. "Hey! They ended camp early 'cause the instructor had an appointment. My bad, I forgot to tell you this morning."

"No problem," Rue said. "I adjusted my hours to make sure I'm home by this time all this week. Did you grab something on the way home?"

"Nah, I'm starving."

As their footsteps approached the living room, I turned to face them.

Cameron rounded the corner, grinning. "Oh, hey, Ms. Alexander!"

"Hey, Cam," I said, smiling.

Rue came in right behind him. "We're just doing some final edits on the grant proposal," he offered casually, grabbing a bottle of water from the fridge like he hadn't just had his hands all over me.

"Cool," Cameron said, then perked up. "Can I heat up the rest of that mac and cheese from last night?"

"Yeah, help yourself. I'm going to start on dinner as soon as we wrap this up."

Leaning against the counter, Rue shot me a small glance as Cameron moved into the kitchen. His jaw pulsed, and his gaze was unreadable.

He didn't seem embarrassed. He looked more... distant. An internal switch had flipped in the last few moments. I *felt* it, like an invisible line was drawn through the house. Through him. I turned back to my laptop. We hadn't crossed the line with Cameron, but we'd gotten close enough for me to see that Rue wouldn't ever let it come that close again.

When we were almost done with the proposal an hour later, I was tired and ready to head home. A long bubble bath and leftover chicken carbonara were calling my name. Then Rue asked me to stay for dinner.

I enjoyed watching him as he moved around the kitchen, stirring the food we'd both helped prepare—garlic shrimp pasta, roasted broccoli, and thick slabs of toasted French bread. His cheerful demeanor had returned, and he seemed over the initial shock of Cameron springing up on us. I sat at the island, unable to resist making additional edits to the proposal.

He wiped a hand on the folded dish towel slung over one shoulder as he peeked in at the bread toasting in the oven. Cameron was upstairs playing an online video game, so it was just us. It all felt familiar in an odd way. Almost like we had all naturally been part of this domestic atmosphere.

"So, I have some final thoughts on the proposal," Rue said, setting the table. "I summarized them in a voice memo the other day. Do you mind listening to it to make sure we got it all in there?"

"Sure, send it over," I said, turning to a fresh page on my notepad.

A few seconds later, my phone buzzed with an AirDrop notification.

Untitled19.m4a

From: Rue's iPad

"Got it," I said, slipping in an AirPod.

"Good," he replied without looking over. "If you don't have any more edits after that, we should be good to go."

"Perfect," I said, tapping play.

The voice in my ear wasn't the polished, confident version of Rue I expected. It was soft. Frayed. He sounded like he was unraveling quietly in the folds of solitude.

"Hey, Low. I need to talk to you. I just don't know what to do. Our lives are starting to overlap more and more. Personal, romantic, and now professional.

I don't know how to handle the way she makes me feel.

She's brilliant. Sweet. She gets me in ways that almost feel scary.

But part of me still needs you to sign off on this somehow.

I know you'd tell me your approval isn't necessary—but I still feel like it is.

It's been years, and I still feel like I'm being disloyal to you. Because I really want her."

His voice was so raw; I could feel his tortured pain in each word. It sent chills through me. My spine went rigid, and my breath barely eased in and out. I didn't dare move. I tried to swallow, but my tongue felt thick and dry.

Just feet away, Rue stirred the sauce and pulled the bread out of the oven. He'd sent me the wrong voice note. And he didn't even know.

My heart tried to process what my brain already knew. This wasn't an old message addressed to his late wife while she was still here. Years after her passing, Rue was still communicating with Willow. *About me.*

"I wish I could talk this through with you. But I feel like I'm betraying everything we had by doing this.

I wish I didn't feel like loving someone new meant loving you less."

I slid the other AirPod in with shaking hands. I needed to hear every word. Even if I didn't *want* to. Even if it cut me to the core.

Cameron walked in and said something that made Rue chuckle. They talked quietly, completely unaware that I was falling apart just ten feet away.

Yet another man you're not good enough for.

The memo still had thirty seconds left, but I paused it. I pulled the AirPods out and tucked them into my purse. I summoned my teacher smile—the wide, practiced one that I could command at a moment's notice, no matter how empty I felt. As I stood, my body felt weightless, like it belonged to someone else. I slid behind the table and took each of their hands, bowing my head for prayer.

Afterward, Rue poured iced tea into three glasses. "Welcome to your first dinner at the Edwards household."

"Thanks for having me," I said, spearing a broccoli floret.

Cameron moaned with delight after his first bite of pasta. "Okay, this is my best meal of the summer. Maybe top two. Uncle Kenny's ribs stand on business."

Rue smiled. "You were just coming off that summer camp food. That'll make anything taste like a five-star meal."

I laughed on cue, even added a little head tilt for drama, but the food was warm, tasteless mush in my mouth.

I watched their blurry silhouettes joke, laugh, clink glasses, and nodded at all the right times. Their words were distant echoes in my ears, yet I smiled when I was expected to. I glanced at my phone in my lap, waiting for the moment that I could politely excuse myself.

When Rue looked over, his gaze was soft, with a hint of concern etched on his handsome features. He reached across the table, placing his hand on mine. I didn't pull away. But I was on fire inside.

When Cam stood to grab dessert, Rue leaned over and whispered, "You good, Tawn?"

I nodded. "Mm-hmm. Just full. Everything was great."

His eyes didn't leave mine until Cameron asked him if they still had ice cream to go with the apple pie. When Rue stood to check the deep freezer, I exhaled.

If this is the beginning of us, I thought, staring down at my half-finished plate, *why do I already feel like the third wheel in my own relationship?*

Chapter 24
Rudolph

It was my week for carpool duty. I dropped off Cam and the other neighborhood chess campers at the school, then headed straight to the site. On the drive over, Glenn's words rang in my head: *Let them take a few hits. If they fail, we'll deal with it. Together.*

Today, I was determined to ease up—to let the crew take the reins while I focused on scouting additional grants for the rec center's professional development programs. I realized Glenn had a point. These were grown men who were capable and well-trained. They could figure their way out of whatever mess came up without me hovering.

When I stepped into the trailer, I blinked at the sight of a full crew already in motion. Then I remembered—I was getting a late start all this week. I was so used to showing up at sunrise, I forgot what it looked like when the site ran without me for a change.

"Morning," I greeted as I made a beeline to the coffee pot.

After pouring my second cup of the day, I slid into my chair behind the desk. The phone was already ringing. Another call.

Another problem. A few minutes later, I slammed the phone back into its cradle hard enough to make the desk rattle. The rec center's HVAC units were flagged as noncompliant in the latest inspection—a minor code variance on paper, but one that could cost us a two-week delay, if not more.

After trying to get the inspector back on the line and leaving two voicemails, I shot off a text to my contact at the city. Next, I filed an appeal through the portal. After two hours, all of it felt like I was shouting into a wind tunnel. No traction. Just static. No matter how careful I was or how proactive I tried to be, something always halted our progress—like I was playing a rigged game of Whack-a-Mole.

Red tape for condos and downtown office spaces was to be expected. So they expected me to treat it like just another contract. They didn't care that it would be an anchor for this neighborhood and for kids who deserved more than leftover resources and broken promises. And now we were stuck. Again.

By the time the crew cleared out and Chase peeled out of the gravel lot—undoubtedly on his way to cop a fresh green smoothie—I knew I wouldn't be going home anytime soon. I relished the peacefulness of the vacant trailer. The sun was slipping below the skyline, and shadows stretched across the drafting table. I sat hunched over the blueprints for the multi-purpose studio, my fingers pressing into the paper as I scanned it for errors that could jeopardize the timeline. Soon, the lines began to swim. I blinked hard, but the blurring didn't subside.

I tried to distract myself by drafting a backup proposal. Maybe if I could re-sequence the demo for the west wing and fast-track drywall installation in the common area, I could make up a week. But only if nobody else dropped the ball. Which wasn't likely now that Glenn wanted me to be Mr. Let-the-Chips-Fall-Where-They-May and trust the same crew that couldn't tell a delivery window from a damn garage door.

I leaned back in my chair, rubbing my forehead. That close call with Tawni the last week hadn't left my mind. Everything felt so right. We learned that we could work together well and were on the exact same page. I was growing optimistic as we relaxed into each other, laughing, and establishing a firm partnership. I'd always known she had her shit together, but I saw a brand new side of her. She was focused and driven. My respect for her bloomed even greater than before. She was so beautiful, sitting there on the couch—soft and carefree. All I wanted to do was lose myself in her.

Until the car door slammed. Reality barged in and reminded me exactly what I was risking. I didn't even think; I just pulled away. Fast. Too fast. Like we'd done something wrong. Tawni had tried to play it off, but I saw the shift in her eyes. I read the hurt and confusion on her face. It wasn't until later that the full weight of the situation settled in. The guilt I felt in that moment didn't make sense. Cam hadn't even seen anything, but I still couldn't breathe right that night. I lay in bed with my eyes wide open, staring at the ceiling fan and hearing *Willow's* final words echoing in my head. *Do right by our son, Rue. That's all I ask.*

How the hell was I supposed to build anything new with someone when I was still terrified to let go of the past? I'd been practically folding in half under pressure in the middle of a project I asked for, freezing up when the woman who'd been my answered prayer leaned in. Doubting myself, a semblance of happiness due to guilt.

My hands were clenched before I realized it. I looked down at my knuckles, and the tremble started to creep in again. I rose to my feet, but it was a little too fast. The chair shrieked as it scraped across the floor. I took a few timid steps toward the mini fridge. Then I backtracked to the door and flipped the lock for some illusion of control. I couldn't afford for anyone to see me like this.

The tension in the back of my neck was coiled tight, like wire. It crept lower, like an invisible hand was squeezing the air out of my lungs. The air thinned out, and I could feel my heart rate quicken. I slumped back into my seat, still trying to inhale deeper. But my breath caught short and grew even more ragged. I leaned forward, pressing my elbows on my knees. I tried to fill my lungs again, but I just couldn't get enough air.

My vision narrowed, and the darkness closed in from the corners like the end scene of a movie. Faint ringing sounded in my ears, and the hum of the overhead lights grew louder, sharper, like static crawling across my scalp.

"What in the world is happening?" I groaned, grabbing the edge of the desk to keep from falling over. My knee bumped against the metal chair leg and sent a sharp clang through the room.

"Focus. Get it together," I willed myself.

But my heart was pounding fast and furious, trying to escape my chest. The air grew thick and hot, but I couldn't move. So I squeezed my eyes shut.

Cam needs you. You can't tap out. You don't get to fall apart. You asked for this, and these kids are relying on you.

A soft knock on the trailer door made me flinch. My hands shook as I reached for the edge of the desk, willing myself to breathe.

"Who is it?" My voice was raw and raspy.

"Rue, it's me." Her voice slipped through the door crack like sunlight through blackout curtains—warm, uninvited... just what I needed.

Relief and aching for her presence and steadiness surged through me. But just as fast, shame tangled itself with my want.

She shouldn't see me like this. Not in this state. I didn't want her here. The person who made me feel light and reminded me I was more than my performance output didn't belong in a space that drained every ounce of peace from me. This was where I unraveled. Where I failed and pretended to be a man with all the answers while barely holding myself together. The last thing I wanted was for her to get tangled in all this heaviness.

How the hell did she even know where to find me? Then I remembered—of course. The grant paperwork. I'd given her the site address weeks ago, back when things felt possible. I just never thought she'd actually show up... like an angel in the dead of my darkness.

"Rue?"

"The key," I finally croaked, "is under the bottom step."

Several moments later, the door unlatched, and I heard hurried footsteps coming toward me. I felt her before I saw her. Her soft and familiar scent wafted in, and her comforting hand rested on my back. She stepped inside cautiously, eyes adjusting to the dim trailer lighting. I'd shut off most of the fluorescents hours ago. Couldn't stand the glare.

"Hey, hey. Rue? Are you okay?"

I shook my head as it hung between my knees.

"Breathe. It's okay. I've got you."

Tawni's voice was calm but confident, which was reassuring. I hated that she was seeing me like this. I hated that I needed her so damn much right now. There was no way I could push her away.

She crouched down in front of me, her palm flat on my back. "Can you match my breath?"

I tried to shake my head, but everything was fuzzy.

"Okay. Just listen to me, okay? I'm right here. You're safe."

I reached out and gripped her wrist, needing to anchor myself.

"Shallow breath in," she whispered, breathing with me. "Shallow breath out. Now try a deeper one. Hold it... now let it go."

I tried. Then I tried again. And again. Finally, the raging storm inside my chest began to subside into gentle ripples. I took in a full pull of air, and it reached the bottom of my lungs. The trembling stopped, and a sense of calm suddenly washed over me.

I sat back and opened my eyes. She was watching me with a steady expression. But her eyes were wet. Despite her best efforts, she couldn't mask the fear on her face. But she stayed. I don't know what I would have done if she hadn't shown up for me.

I wanted to thank her. My arms longed to pull her close. I needed to tell her I was okay. But shame engulfed me. The shame of what she witnessed and how much I needed her to help me get through it. The shame that I couldn't even protect my son from the mess of who I was. The pressure I placed on him and myself underneath the demands of high expectations. It all surged to the surface at once. I couldn't succumb to it, so all I was left with was anger.

"Look," I finally said, "I know what this looks like. But I just needed a minute to catch my breath."

Tawni's eyes didn't budge from mine. "You're having a panic attack."

"I had one," I corrected, jaw clenched. "It's over now."

"You're still in it."

Her voice was gentle, but it felt like a spotlight. And I hated how much she saw.

I pulled back and stood on shaky legs, brushing past her toward the mini fridge for a bottle of water.

"Why did you come by?" I asked before opening the bottle and draining nearly half of it in one gulp.

"I wanted to drop off a copy of the letter of support from my superintendent. You didn't answer my text."

"It's been a long day. I must've missed it. You could have just emailed it."

She paused. "I could have. Look, Rue... it's okay to have a moment. We all do."

I let out a hollow laugh before draining the bottle. Not an option for me. Not when I was the only one holding the line. I wanted to tell her that I was fine and could handle it all. That I didn't need her. I dropped onto a small bench by the back wall, elbows on my knees, fingers rubbing my temples.

She sat across from me with pleading eyes. "I want to be here," she said.

"But I don't want you to be."

Her brow knit. "Rue—"

"No," I snapped, louder than I meant to. "You're not my damn wife, Tawni."

The words shot out of me, jagged and bitter. Her mouth parted slightly, but she didn't speak. Silence fell between us—dense and unmoving. Tawni's shoulders tensed, and her hands, which had been loosely clasped in front of her, slowly released. One dropped to her side, the other brushing against her thigh. Her gaze faltered, drifting past me, then back. When she finally focused on me again, it was like she'd physically pulled back. Something drew inside her that I wasn't meant to see anymore.

And still, she didn't speak.

No longer able to stomach the pain in her eyes, I looked away. "I didn't mean it like that. I just... I don't know what's happening. I'm trying to keep this damn project from falling apart, trying to be everything for everyone, and I can't even open a damn email these days without it causing me to break into a sweat."

"You don't have to be everything," she said. "Not for me."

"I know. But I *wanted* to be."

The silence stretched on and on.

"Look, you should really go," I said finally. "I need to pull my thoughts together, and Cam's waiting for me at home."

She stood slowly. I didn't look up.

"Okay. I'll check in with you tomorrow," she said.

I didn't answer her. Not because I didn't want her to. I just didn't trust my voice at the moment.

When the door clicked shut behind her, the heavy and familiar weight returned, coupled with my guilt. I'd hurt her. Pushed away the only person who'd shown up for me. I leaned back, staring at the ceiling. This wasn't just about work anymore. I had to heed the needs of my mental health and preserve my peace. I didn't need to be saved.

But maybe I didn't have to suffer alone either.

Chapter 25
Tawni

I didn't know what I expected when I walked into the trailer, but it sure as hell wasn't Rue—hunched over, trembling, barely able to catch a breath.

My heart dropped at the sight of his body trembling as he grappled with fear. I had never seen him in a state anything close to that. That's exactly what motivated me into action. I did what anyone would do for someone they care about. I stayed, letting him hold onto me. I let him know that he was safe and that it would all be okay—even if I didn't know it for sure.

For a brief, quiet moment... it seemed like he believed me. His grip softened, and he finally let go of that shallow, frantic breathing. When he pulled in a full breath, I watched the panic drain from his face. But it was slowly replaced by sheer exhaustion. When shame crept in like a shadow, all the softness we'd just shared was cloaked in darkness.

He immediately pulled away and stood up, dismissive like he hadn't just unraveled in front of me. Watching him grow cold and quiet before my eyes was heartbreaking. It wasn't until he asked why I came that I realized he'd barely even looked at me. It was jarring to be asked the reason for my presence as if it needed to be justified. He'd never done that before.

I gave him the truth. I'd dropped off the superintendent's recommendation letter. I'd stayed up revising our executive summary three nights in a row because we were building something together. At least I thought.

When he gave that bullshit reason for ignoring my text, I let it slide for the sake of trying to tread lightly. He still needed room to breathe, and he was hurting. So I led him to a chair and tried again to help him relax. I wasn't going to give up on him. Not when I'd just seen him struggling in a state of panic all alone in a trailer.

Then, he hit me with: *"You can just leave. You're not my damn wife, Tawni."*

It didn't register at first. Probably because my brain fought against it. Surely I'd misheard him. Surely he didn't mean it that way. But the way he avoided my eyes said everything. His jaw was clenched like he knew he'd crossed a line but wasn't about to walk it back. He didn't even flinch.

I was amazed at how those hurtful words fell from his lips so easily. He delivered them without warning or hesitation. Serving up a clean, sharp slap of reality that cracked a part of me I didn't even know was still tender and unhealed.

But he didn't dare repeat it. He didn't need to. The steely look in his eyes, accompanied by the thick silence that hung in the air afterward, confirmed everything for me. This man was in a dark place. His posture shifted, and he could no longer hold my gaze. Oh yeah, he meant that shit.

I'd just helped him through a terrifying moment, and just moments later, he was making me feel like I was an intruder. I'd driven across town, found the key when he didn't even have the strength to come unlock the door, and knelt on that cold, filthy floor with him, whispering breath into his petrified lungs. But none of it had changed what he saw when he looked at me. I was a substitute. A stand-in for a memory he wouldn't let go of. A pitiful reminder of a life he couldn't rebuild.

I gathered my things slowly, my hands moving on instinct because my heart was frozen in place. I needed to get out of there before my tears said what my voice couldn't. When I stepped outside, the warm evening air still felt cool against my hot cheeks. I stalked back to my car, started the engine, and sat staring at the streetlights shining straight ahead. I had shown up for him and made sure he had everything he needed. Because this man literally had no one else checking on him. Why would they, when he constantly insisted he was okay?

I was just a tool to him. A permanent stand-in for someone who wasn't coming back—a distraction he could parade around. All so no one would notice that he wasn't healing. The truth was, healing wasn't yet possible for Rue.

Because he hadn't even managed to stop the bleeding yet.

Chapter 26
Rudolph

When I pulled into the driveway, I instinctively reached down to lower the music volume so I wouldn't disturb my neighbors. Then I realized I'd driven home in silence. I lifted the large pepperoni pizza and buffalo wings off the seat. Cameron was already at my car door, yanking it open before I could even step out.

"Is that what I think it is?" he asked, his eyes locked on the red-and-white checkered box.

"Yep. It's officially pizza and wing night," I said, holding it up like a trophy. "And no, I didn't forget the garlic butter sauce this time."

He raised an eyebrow, skeptical. "Okay, who are you and what have you done with Dad?"

I smirked and nudged him back inside. "Don't make me rethink this whole 'cool dad' moment."

We settled on the couch, the box between us, slices of pizza drooping over our laps, sans plates. I opened the 2-liter of Pepsi and handed it over.

"We're actually eating in here?" Cameron asked, mid-bite.

"On the couch? No paper plates? No lecture about crumbs or saucy fingers?"

I shrugged and grabbed a wing. "I wouldn't get used to it."

"Nah, Dad. This is sus. Are you love-drunk or sumthin'?"

I almost choked. "Boy, just eat your food."

He cackled and flopped back into the cushions, the opening credits of a stand-up special flickering on the screen. For a while, it was perfect. Laughter, good food, and bonding with my favorite person.

Twenty minutes later, my phone buzzed. I looked down and saw my sister's name on the screen. I let it go to voicemail. When it buzzed again, panic shot through me. Chandler never called back to back. Was something going on with Mom? I wiped my hand on a napkin and answered on the third ring.

"Hey sis, what's up?" I asked, my tone clipped.

She didn't respond right away. Just breathed.

I was instantly on my feet. "Chan? What's going on?"

Her voice came out snarky. "I just had the worst date of my life."

I released a breath. "What happened?"

"Remember the guy I was telling you about? Who I met online? We finally met up for drinks. Everything was good whenever we FaceTimed. He looked just like his picture. So I thought we were in the clear. But halfway through the date, I notice he's... different. Arrogant. Kept criticizing what I was wearing and how much I talk. Then, he stands up and says, 'I'm going to the bathroom. Be right back,' and doesn't come back. He ordered three appetizers and two drinks, then left me with the check."

I started pacing. "Where are you?"

"On my third drink, sitting at the bar."

"Chandler."

"I just needed a minute before I went home."

I grabbed my keys. "Send me the location."

I was so busy putting on my shoes, I didn't notice she paused at first.

"Rue, I just called you to vent. I don't—"

"Never mind. I just checked it. You're at ACE's. I'm already on the way."

Cameron watched me grab my wallet and keys. "Everything okay?"

"I'm gonna check on Auntie Chandler real quick."

"You want me to roll with you?"

"Nah. Stay here and finish the movie. Don't eat all them wings, boy."

"Too late." He burped, grinning with a face covered in sauce.

* * *

ACE's was a small neighborhood bar that wasn't far from my house. I parked across the street at a meter, my jaw tightening as I approached the bar, spotting Chandler through the window. She was sitting on a high stool, talking expressively. The bartender was nodding while wiping down glasses, listening with a patience likely perfected over time.

As I hit the door, I spotted him. He was easy to recognize from the picture Chandler had sent over last week. He stuck out like a sore thumb with a mohawk that was dyed bronze, a flannel shirt, and Timbs like it wasn't 76 degrees outside. He was laughing with another dude, sitting near the corner like he hadn't just humiliated my sister.

I headed toward him. Chandler shook her head slightly and pleaded, "Don't, Rue."

But it was too late. I stormed up to his table, swirling my car keys on my finger. "You the one who thought it was cool to leave a woman alone at a bar, stuck paying your bill?"

He blinked, his mouth hanging open for a moment. Then he glanced over at his boy. Suddenly, he found his voice. "Who the hell are you?"

I stepped closer. "I'm her brother."

He raised his hands, cocky. "It was a trash-ass date, man. I suggest you mind your business and get out of here."

Chandler walked up behind me, murmuring my name. She grabbed my arm, trying to pull me back toward the bar. But I couldn't. Not yet.

"I don't care what the date was like. You don't disrespect women." I said, counting off on my fingers. "You don't expect a woman to pick up your tab. And you *damn sure* don't act like she doesn't exist by sitting your dumb ass at a table less than 50 feet away."

"This dude." He smirked, elbowing his friend before turning back to me. "Thanks for the lesson, little man. You gon' teach me some more manners for dog-walking your big sis? Fuck is this? Sesame Street?"

He turned to look at his friend again, who just shook his head. Before he could turn back around, I grabbed his collar and dragged him clean out of his chair. I used his weight to send him crashing back against the wall hard enough to shake the bricks.

"Who's the little man now, huh?" My teeth were clenched, but spittle still landed on his cheek.

He laughed, nervous now.

I cocked back my arm, my fist aimed at his face.

"Okay, okay. You got it, big man."

"Apologize to her. Right now."

"Alright! I'm sorry, damn."

My chest heaved, but I kept my tone even and low. "Look at her. Say her name."

He glanced over at Chandler. I couldn't see her expression because I was too busy hoisting this sorry example of a man in the air. His Timbs were dangling as he wriggled in my grasp.

"I'm sorry, Chandler. For disrespecting you. I shouldn't have done you like that. I'll pay you back for our food and drinks."

I released him, and he slumped back onto the floor. His ankle rolled, and he lost his balance for a second. When he caught himself, he took a step back from me, breathing hard.

Chandler grabbed my arm, pleading. "Okay, Rue. Let's go."

I glanced over at his friend to see if he wanted some too, but he hadn't even moved from his spot. When I looked at the bartender, he was still cleaning glasses. "Yo man, I don't blame you for what you did. Guy's an asshole. But you need to leave before someone calls the cops."

I nodded and guided Channy out of the bar. "Let's go."

I ushered my sister out the door. We headed to my car, and after she slid inside, she was quiet.

"I didn't call you for that," she said after a few moments.

"Then what'd you call me for?" I muttered, staring ahead.

She looked over at me. "To have a few laughs over a clown-ass dude. Like we always do."

I shrugged. "Well, I guess I wasn't in a laughing mood tonight."

She snorted. "He was at least three inches taller, and you lifted him smooth off his feet."

I shook my head. "Light work. Especially for talking reckless about you."

Her hand settled on my forearm. "Rue, that wasn't just about me."

I didn't answer.

She exhaled. "You snapped. And I'm not saying he didn't deserve a warning, but you went straight from zero to sixty. That's not you."

I stared out into the dark parking lot, my chest tight. "I don't know what's wrong with me."

She turned in her seat. "You do. You're just not ready to say it out loud."

After a few moments of silence, she gently asked, "Are things still good on the job? With Cam and Tawni?"

I swallowed. "I hurt her. On purpose."

Her brows lifted, but she didn't jump in to fill the silence.

"I don't even know why I keep doing this. Pushing people away. Blowing up. I feel like I'm always holding back this flood, and tonight..." I shook my head. "I cracked."

She let that land, then her tone was soft when she said, "You've been through a lot, Rue. You lost Willow. You've been pushed into a single father role. And through it all, you put your head down and kept going. But stuffing down all that grief and pressure doesn't make it disappear. It just builds. And then somebody says the wrong thing in a bar—and boom."

I pressed my thumb into my temple. "I'm failing at everything. At work, at home, with Tawni... I keep lashing out like I'm protecting something, but I'm just scared."

"You're allowed to be scared," she said, her tone steady. "But you're not allowed to use fear as an excuse to hurt people who care about you. You're so much better than that, little bro."

I nodded slowly.

"You gotta fix this, Rue," she said. "Not just with Tawni. With yourself. For yourself."

I met her eyes for the first time since we got in the car. "Sis, I'm trying."

She gave me a small smile. "Good. Then start there."

* * *

At first, I blamed it all on the anxiety meds. I'd convinced myself that adjusting the dosage was what had made me pull away, shut down, and fade to black. But the more time I spent wrestling with the truth, the more I realized I'd been justifying leaning into the fog I was already drifting toward. I told myself the silence was about tapping out and tapping into myself. Gaining clarity and slowing down before things spun out. But it felt more like drowning with my eyes open.

The morning after Tawni walked out of the trailer, I called Glenn.

"You sure about this?" he asked, not bothering to hide the concern in his voice.

I was, for once. I told him I needed to step away—not for a long lunch or for a day, but really step back. That I wouldn't be checking my laptop, replying to emails, or even taking work calls for a full two weeks. Chase would have to take the lead, and whatever direction the team decided to go from there, I would respect it. I'd made it clear: this wasn't just about emotional burnout. This was about honoring my mental health and protecting my peace. Because I'd risked imploding while trying to hold everyone else's world together.

Tawni's name and smiling picture kept lighting up my screen. Text messages and voicemails that I could barely bring myself to listen to.

Hey, can you review the final budget draft tonight? I got an extension, but the hard deadline is noon tomorrow.

Rue, are you okay? I haven't heard from you. Just let me know if I should submit without you.

Seriously. Did I do something wrong?

Then nothing. Her silence screamed louder than all the pings I'd ignored. I stared at the phone until it went black again. And still, I couldn't move. Falling for her was too easy. No matter how hard I tried to fight it, she'd pulled me in. The whole time, I wondered, what if I wasn't stable enough? Healed enough? Present enough? Half of me was still trapped in the recesses of my tortured past. I wanted to give her more than the jagged pieces I hadn't glued back together yet. She deserved wholeness. And I still had work to do.

But God, I missed her.

The days all bled into each other, and I kept telling myself I'd respond to her tomorrow. I'd feel better in the morning. If I could just stop the thoughts from racing long enough to sleep, maybe I'd have the strength to try again. But sleep didn't come easy. And when I was finally able to grasp it, it slipped between my fingertips like sand, restless and haunted.

I dreamed of Tawni. My tortured mind had conjured her—vivid and beautiful, reaching for me with that smile that once lit up my life. When she began walking away, I stood frozen, unable to follow her. Guilt plagued me because I was the one who asked her to believe in me. To build something with me. Now she was alone, waiting for me to fulfill that promise. But I was too busy sitting in my own wreckage, hoping silence could shield us both from the pain of disappointment.

* * *

Cameron picked up on the shift right away. He didn't say anything at first. I noticed him hovering around me more, like he was afraid I'd disappear if he blinked.

I was sitting on the couch, scrolling, though my eyes saw nothing.

"What's up, Dad? Are you mad at her or something?"

I looked up. I hadn't even realized he'd plopped down beside me. "Mad at who?"

He rolled his eyes. "Ms. Alexander. You guys don't hang out anymore. And you're not as happy."

I tried to force a smile, but I couldn't even fool myself, let alone a cynical pre-teen. "I'm fine, Cam. It's just complicated adult stuff."

Cameron picked at a loose thread on his hoodie. "You're not gonna break her heart, are you?"

I bristled. His tone was protective, authoritative. His pointed stare sliced straight through me.

"Son, I..." I whispered. I wanted to offer him some type of encouragement. To let him know that that was the last thing I wanted to do to her. But I was physically and emotionally exhausted with nothing left to give. I was numb, empty.

Cameron stood and walked away. He didn't crack one of his jokes or call me dramatic. He just left me, and all I could do was watch, too rooted in the misery I'd created to stop him.

A few nights later, I heard him playing video games in his room. I was about to head to my room when I heard quiet sniffles, just like when his mom died and he didn't want me to hear.

I knocked. "Cam?"

When there was no answer, I cracked the door open. The game was still going, but he was on his bed, facing the wall, curled in a fetal position.

"Cam, are you feeling okay?" I asked, rushing to his bed.

"I'm fine," he mumbled.

I sat beside him. "No, you're not. Please tell me what's wrong."

We sat in silence for a few minutes.

Then I heard him whisper, "You're shutting me out. You feel far away again."

I closed my eyes, tilting my head back. I'd gotten so used to shouldering grief that I didn't realize how it impacted those around me. I reached for his shoulder. "Cam, I'm sorry. I'm right here. And you can talk to me whenever you need to. Nothing's more important than you."

"How are you gonna fix it?" he asked, still facing the wall.

I didn't know what he meant—fix it with Tawni? With him? Or fix *me*? It all felt so tangled I could feel myself starting to retreat again. But I owed him more than a shell of myself.

Before I could answer, he spoke again, his voice barely above a whisper.

"A friend from school sent me a video from the night of the music festival," he said. "It was of you and Tawni... dancing together."

I blinked, staring at his back while he talked. My mind went back to the night of the festival, when Tawni had frozen, looking off at something in the distance while we were on the dance floor. She'd seen him recording us.

He shifted on his pillow, finally facing me. "Don't worry, he's a good friend, and he promised to delete it after sending it to me."

I swallowed hard. "How did seeing that make you feel?"

"It was hella weird at first," he said with an awkward laugh. "But I kept watching it over and over. 'Cause seeing you smile like that. Being happy and just carefree... was everything."

I nodded. *It was everything for me, too.*

"It made me happy," he added, leaning on his arm. "Because I knew you weren't just pretending for me. You were really having fun again. Living again."

I turned my full body toward him, my heart thudding.

He continued. "I've never really said anything about this, but... I'm starting to lose memories of Mom. It scares me because I try my best to hold on tight, but I'm starting to forget things like how her voice sounded and what her perfume smelled like. But I do remember enough to know what made her special."

I took in a shaky breath, struggling to hold it together.

"And when I've been around Tawni lately, I start to have some of those feelings again. Like maternal."

Tawni. He'd called her Tawni for the first time, not Ms. Alexander.

He laid a hand on my arm, his eyes glassy but steady. "She reminds me of the parts of Mom that made me feel safe. That I miss the most. The parts that make me feel like I can just be a kid again."

Conviction hit me like a ton of bricks. I was too hard on him. My expectations of him didn't leave him much room for just being a kid. My throat tightened. I nodded to let him know I was still listening, even though it took everything in me to hold back my sobs.

He looked up at me with Willow's eyes, and it almost wrecked me. "I want her in our lives, Dad. I know it's what's best. And I think you do too."

I nodded and pulled him in for a hug that lasted several long minutes. I was unsure of what I was silently promising him. But that just meant I had to address all three priorities at once—Tawni, Cam, and finally, myself.

Chapter 27
Tawni

I stepped out of the yoga dome on loose and limber legs, but my heart still felt heavy. Two weeks had passed since I'd left a letter taped to Rue's front door. I let him know about the voice memo he'd mistakenly sent after I finally stopped pretending I could wait forever for him to get back to me.

The wind lightly stirred up the scent of lavender and eucalyptus still clinging to my skin from my morning massage. I crossed the gravel path toward the wraparound porch of the bed-and-breakfast. Tiff and Trish were already there, curled up on rocking chairs with mugs in hand, their faces glowing with serenity from their sound bath.

"Well, you look like your chakras may have been *slightly* realigned," Trish teased, patting the chair beside her.

I plopped down with a sigh, pulling the blanket around my legs. "I didn't quite see my ancestors or anything, but I definitely experienced serious clarity during savasana."

Tiff passed me a mug of green tea. "That's what happens when you slow down long enough to hear your own thoughts."

Nodding, I took a slow sip and let the quietness wrap around us. "Jaclyn had to leave?"

Trish nodded. "Yeah, she left a note on your bed. It was good hanging out with her. She's cool."

As I stirred my tea, I thought back to the previous night, just before we all turned in for bed. Jaclyn and I had ended up on the back patio together, the fire pit burning low between us.

She'd looked out into the woods for a long time before finally speaking. "Tawn... I know I gave you a hard time about dating Rue. And I stand by what I said, but... I don't want you to think I don't believe in you."

I pulled the blanket tighter around my shoulders, looking up at the starry sky.

"What you've been going through," she said, her voice low. "It's heavy. That man, that situation... all of it is complicated. And I know you probably think I've just been sitting back waiting to say 'I told you so.' But that's not what this is."

Surprised by her words, I turned in my chair to face her.

"It's not easy watching you hurt," she continued. "Especially when I want to protect you but I know I can't just fix it for you. Like I always did when we were kids."

I snorted. "You mean like that time you stormed outside with your head full of pink foam rollers because you heard me play-fighting with a girl from down the street?"

Jaclyn rolled her eyes but chuckled. "Sis, you were screaming like she'd body-slammed you. Shit, I thought it was go time. Had Vaseline on my face and everything."

"Go where? You ran out wearing house shoes, Jac."

"And they didn't stop me from coming down that porch poised and ready to drag a child. I was fully committed to the cause," she doubled down.

We had a tense stare-off for a moment before bursting into easy laughter.

As it slowly faded, I turned to really look at her. I wasn't used to seeing vulnerability on her face.

"Until recently, I was a little jealous," she added after a beat. "Of Tiff and Trish. What do y'all call yourselves? Triple Threat? It felt like anytime something big happened in your life —good or bad—you turned to them first. I took that personally for a long time."

I opened my mouth to respond, but she waved it off.

"But I get it now," she said. "I've been watching y'all today. They've been giving you space and time to just feel without jumping in to fix things. As the Vaseline moment proves, I've never really been good at that. I can be a little quick to judge and throw my advice out there. But I wanna get better. I don't wanna be the kind of sister you just *have*, but one you can count on."

My throat tightened. I'd been waiting to hear those words from her for half of my life.

"I'm glad you asked me to come here," she continued, her voice barely above a whisper. "I really needed this time with you."

I didn't have a speech or the perfect response to offer my sister at that moment. So I just leaned into her side, resting my head on her shoulder like when we were kids. Before things got complicated and life got in the way of our friendship. This time, we didn't need pretty little words to get it right.

Now, sitting on the porch with Trish and Tiff, the memory lingered with fondness and love. Jaclyn may have left this morning, but our conversation stayed with me. We were finally starting to respect each other as women who were flawed, heal-ing, and still figuring out our lives.

"Yeah, she's been super supportive, helping me with all of the marketing and promo items for the showcase," I said, giving my tea another stir.

"Speaking of which, DJ Luxx agreed to emcee, so there's a good chance your single *Under October Moonlight* will be played on the radio."

"What?"

We shot to our feet, squealing so loud, we scared the owner's dog, who was resting on the porch a few feet away. We lowered our voices, locking hands and jumping with glee. After processing the good news and settling back into our chairs, we took time to enjoy the scenic view in front of us. The sun was descending behind the trees, and the sky blushed orange. I was grateful for all the opportunities unfolding for me, but my mind was still a million miles away.

"I wrote Rue a letter, y'all," I admitted, still gazing ahead.

I felt them both grow still beside me.

"I left it on his door a couple of weeks ago."

When I looked up, four wide brown eyes were fixed on me. Neither of them moved or said anything. I knew they were afraid to. After Rue's meltdown in the trailer, I'd mostly kept to myself. If it weren't for my girlfriends practically kidnapping me and booking this trip for a few days, I'd still be under the covers. They'd been handling me with patience and care for the past day, but I owed them an explanation for my radio silence. So I finally shared the details of what occurred between Rue and me at the trailer earlier that morning. Now, I was ready to give them the rest of the story. The full story.

"I let him know I received the wrong voice memo. The one where he basically called me 'confusing' and said I was making him feel something he wasn't ready for." I tried to keep the bitterness from my tone. "I can't believe he's still been talking to Willow after three years."

Trish reached over and touched my knee. "Tawn, that had to be hard to learn about it the way you did."

"I had an idea that he was still struggling with her death," I sighed. "But I just needed to hear it, even if he didn't mean for me to."

"I'm sure it was devastating, but maybe knowing about it is for the best," Tiff said, leaning in. "What did you say in the letter?"

"That I get that grief doesn't instantly end just because someone new shows up. I told him I wasn't angry. Just... sad that he didn't think I was worth having a conversation with. I'm disappointed that he felt like he needed to cover up how he's been coping while in pain. In silence. How he's been lying to himself and the people he loves."

Trish said, "You're feelings are valid, sis. I would have felt the same way."

I squeezed her hand. "Thanks, girl. I also told him I'd be stepping back. I feel like he's partly been using our relationship as a way to prove to himself that he's recovered. But I'm not auditioning for a role that still hasn't been vacated. I recognize and respect that Willow was his wife and she'll always have a place in his heart. In his life. But he hasn't come to terms with the fact that she isn't able to play an *active* role in his life anymore."

Tiff's eyes shone with tears. "That's so heavy, friend."

"I love him," I admitted, my voice cracking. "I don't think I realized it until that moment. Because of how much power he had... to hurt me."

Tears flowed—silent, steady, and cleansing. Trish rummaged in her crossbody for a moment, then pressed a tissue into my palm, and I wiped my eyes. After taking a shaky breath, I continued. "But I love myself smore. And I have to stop waiting for a version of him to emerge that isn't ready to show up."

"Sis, it may have been hard as hell for you to give him the

space he needed," Trish said softly, "but you did. Even if it tore you apart."

I nodded again. "It did. But after being torn open, I stood firm in my boundaries. A part of me has stopped seeing respect as something I had to earn. After everything I've been for him, it's something I'm due. With respect comes truth, communication, and honor."

Tiff tilted her head. "Say that shit."

Trish leaned over and looked me in the eye. "You didn't just walk away. You took another step *toward* yourself: the woman who knows exactly what she needs and what she doesn't."

Her words landed on my chest and stood on it with a weight that left me breathless. Boundaries can be so painful to enforce, but I was learning that they feel so damn good to stand behind. Thinking about how Rue used hostility to mask his vulnerability during his emotional crisis hurt me to the core. Why couldn't he just take that moment to open up? Hadn't I earned his trust by now?

"And... since I'm laying things bare," I said, eyes fixed on a knot in the porch railing, "I've got something I need to confess."

Both of them stilled, probably thinking *what more could she have to tell us?*

"I told y'all I ended things with Dante—and I did. But... I wasn't as 'done' as I claimed to be," I said, flexing my fingers around my mug. "A few months after our breakup, we slipped... quite a few times. Nothing official, just at times when I was lonely or craving familiarity. I was focused on my growth, but I still had some weak moments."

Tiff nodded with a slow blink. "So it was purely physical. Not about getting back with him?"

"No. And it was all on me. I stopped trusting the process. There were times when I strongly doubted that someone like Rue would ever come along to understand me... nonetheless *choose* me. I can admit now that I kept pieces of myself hidden after we broke up. Even from y'all. I admit to being the secret squirrel you accuse me of being." I winked at Tiff'.

"Hey, we all have to keep a little for ourselves sometimes," she said with a shrug.

"Dante felt safe even though I knew he wasn't good for me," I admitted.

Tiff smiled. "Sis, that's not failure. It's fear of leaving what's familiar behind for the unknown. It's all part of the healing journey. And that path is curvy and rocky as hell. The most important thing to recognize is, you're not there anymore."

I nodded as Trish leaned over and wiped my tears. "I see that now. And I'm sorry for not being honest with you. The burden of hiding that part of me from y'all was almost unbearable." I released a shaky breath and smiled. "But now I understand that I was getting him out of my system to prepare myself for something better."

Trish pointed at me. "*Someone* better. The healed version of yourself. We see her. And exactly how hard she fought to be here."

"Thanks, Trish," I said, leaning in to accept a long hug from her.

"You know," I said, settling back into my rocking chair. "I always thought love was supposed to involve tremendous sacrifice. If I wasn't staying, waiting, or proving myself, then what was I in it for? But real love—*healthy* love—means knowing when to stay and when to walk away with grace."

Trish nodded, reaching over to squeeze my hand. "But grace doesn't protect you from the hurt. So we're here to check in, sis. How are you feeling?"

"I mean, it hurt like hell to hear him on that recording, pouring his heart out to someone who wasn't me," I whispered, then took in a shallow breath. "Distancing myself when I know he doesn't have anyone else that can give him what I can. But I can't be that same woman who used to burn herself out just to keep someone else happy. Not even for a man as amazing as Rue."

"Hell, not for anyone," Tiff added, rocking and sipping.

Silence fell over us again, and we allowed the moment to stretch wide. The wind whistled in the trees as we lost ourselves in our collective thoughts.

"I really hope he finds peace," I finally said. "After all he's been through, he deserves that. And I hope whatever he's going through leads him somewhere safe to heal and grow."

Tiff let a beat pass before she leaned over and asked, "And if he doesn't find peace?"

I smiled faintly. "Then I'll keep focusing on what I'm doing. Building peace for myself."

Trish leaned back and stretched. "Oh, this retreat was exactly what you needed. Hell, what *we* all needed."

"Most definitely," I agreed. "It's nice to be reminded that there's still purpose in the pause. I needed this softness and a space where I can hurt and still be whole. I'm just excited to get back to me."

As we caught up on each other's lives, the sun disappeared and the first stars began to dot the sky. In the quiet moments between our laughter, something loosened in me. I knew that I was far from getting closure on my situation with Rue. But I was grateful to finally get something even better. I was seeing my life with fresh clarity—clear on what I needed, and even clearer on what I expected from others.

Chapter 28
Rudolph

The envelope was still in the top drawer in my kitchen. Soft around the corners from being wedged in the doorframe too long. Cameron had brought it in with him one day after chess camp after finding it stuck there on his way inside. I snatched it from his hands before he could ask questions—form any sense of hope about us. Because one look at the scripty handwriting and I already knew who it was from. But I hadn't opened it. Maybe it was procrastination. It could be denial or just plain neglect of my feelings and hers. Either way, it stayed buried in that drawer for weeks. Now, as I finally found the courage to pull it free and face what she had to say, my stomach flipped. Because I knew it wasn't a love letter. It was the ending I'd been pretending wouldn't come. Whatever was waiting for me inside was a goodbye.

I stood there in the middle of my kitchen, unmoving, the silence collecting around me was thick with guilt. Cameron was down the street at a friend's house, thank God. I couldn't let him see me unravel. I knew if it were ever to happen, Tawni was the only one capable of doing it. I peeled it open with trembling hands and began to read. By the second paragraph, my throat burned from holding back my emotions. By the third, my legs began to weaken, and I had to sit down.

She'd heard it. The memo. The one I never meant for anyone to hear—especially not her. I'd recorded it on the way to work, half-awake and fully overwhelmed. It was supposed to be a vent session. Something to delete after getting it off my chest. But I'd sent it to her instead. And then I'd vanished. She hadn't chased me, just sent a letter. Her words were careful. Gentle, sweet, and thoughtful.

I'd ghosted her while she was hurting, confused, and heartbroken.

The realization sat in my chest like cement. I thought I'd been giving myself space to process everything—but I'd actually been hiding. Yet, Tawni had still given me the grace I didn't even have the courage to ask for. I stared down at the letter, the words blurring together as I realized I owed her more than silence. I owed her the truth. But first, I needed to face it myself. There was no other way.

I opened the voice memo app. I wasn't ready—but I pressed play anyway. I hit play.

"I don't know what I'm doing. She's... confusing. Not in a bad way. Just in that way where you think you're safe and then suddenly you're not. And I hate that part of me that still desperately needs to talk to you. I hate that I still ask your permission to move forward with my life."

I paused it. My voice sounded small, like someone I didn't know. Strained with distance and exhaustion. Laced with regret and shame. Like a man trying to outpace his grief but stumbling over every memory instead. How had I expected Tawni to hold all of that?

I covered my mouth with my hand and sat there in silence. I wasn't ready to call her. I didn't want to say all the right things now only to lose her again. I wanted to be ready to prove every word of it. But I also knew I couldn't get there alone. She had an opening tomorrow. The relief hit hard—so intense it nearly knocked the wind out of me.

I scrolled through my contacts until I found Dorian's name. The one person who always called me on my shit and stayed anyway.

He picked up on the second ring. "Hey, man. Everything good?"

"No," I said quietly. "Not really. You got a minute?"

We sat on the phone for close to an hour. I told him everything. About the memo. The silence. The letter. The regret that had perched under my ribs, triggering anguish that I'd refused to acknowledge.

Dorian didn't interrupt much, but when he did, it mattered. "You were honest," he said. "Even if it wasn't meant for her ears, that message came from a real place."

"Yeah, but it wasn't fair to her," I muttered.

"It wasn't," he agreed. "But Rue, you've been grieving with one foot stuck in the past and one toe dipped in the future. That's a tormented way to live."

His candor knocked me off balance. Because he was right. I'd built a whole new house in quicksand and called it progress.

"Remember when your therapist had you writing letters to Willow?" he asked.

I nodded, even though he couldn't see me. "Yeah. That really helped. For a while."

"Until it didn't?"

"Until I needed something quicker. More immediate access to relief." I exhaled. "That's when I started the voice memos."

Dorian was quiet for a second. "You ever wonder if the reason you stopped writing was because letters felt too... final?"

I rubbed my temples. When I finally spoke, my voice caught, "I just didn't want to let her go, man."

"So you didn't. You kept the lifeline open through those memos."

"I thought it was helping me cope."

"Maybe it did for a while," he said gently. "But it's been keeping you stuck, bro."

Quicksand. I closed my eyes. The silence between us was thick. I let it settle for a moment, needing more time before I could find the strength to agree with him.

"I think I'm finally ready, bro," I whispered. "To move on."

He let a few beats pass before saying the one thing I didn't know I needed to hear:

"That's exactly what my sister would want for you, Rue."

I believed him with every ounce of hope I had left. Because the weight of carrying her, clutching her with all of my might, began to ease. My memories didn't fade, and my vision of her didn't disappear.

But the loosening of her hold around my heart finally allowed me to breathe.

* * *

The evening sky blushed, pink at the edges as I got in the car and began driving with nowhere to go. Several minutes later, I looked around, surprised to find myself pulling into the park. I guess my heart had led me here.

The lake looked like melted steel, stretching into the horizon. Muscle memory guided me past the trail markers and the familiar bends in the gravel path until I reached the bench I was looking for. Our bench.

The first time Willow and I stumbled across this overlook, we were arguing. It was about something stupid that I don't even remember. We'd stopped here and sat in silence for a long time, each too stubborn to apologize, neither of us wanting to walk away.

Then she reached for my hand and said, "Rue, we don't have to agree on everything to love each other."

After that, this park bench became our place. It was where we came to decompress, reset, and dream out loud. We built our life here. It was where I'd proposed to her. It was the place we brought Cameron during his colicky moments as a newborn when we were each deprived of sleep. It was the backdrop for our first family picture and the exact spot we'd taken him fishing for the first time.

After she passed... this place became my quiet refuge. Where no one could ever find me. Because it was somewhere only we knew. Just the three of us.

After a few minutes, I stood and walked over to the small bridge. I leaned against the railing with my eyes fixed on the water, waiting for the throbbing ache in my chest to dull.

"Cam's growing up fast," I said. "You'd be so proud. He's figuring things out, just like you said. Armed with the perfect mix of your curiosity and my stubbornness."

The breeze off the lake stirred the trees around me, but no answers came. They never did. Still, I kept talking.

"I'm trying to be the best me I can, Low. I really am. I'm taking vitamins, drinking water, and exercising. The bills are paid. And I'm showing up. Every single day. But if I'm being honest, sometimes it feels like I'm just pretending to have it all together for Cam's sake."

I dragged a hand down my face.

"I still think about you. More often than I probably should. And talking to you like this, hoping you'll show up with a sign or something, is still part of my daily life. But lately, it's felt different. Foreign."

The next words caught in my throat. "There's someone new."

Just saying it out loud caused guilt to rush in, riddling my skin, but I pressed on.

"She's nothing like you," I chuckled, letting the memory of Tawni's bold laughter wash over me. "But she's kind. She listens. She sees everything. Even the parts I try to keep well hidden."

I paused, dreading to utter my next words.

"Low, I want to see where this goes with Tawni. But I can't keep standing here with one foot shackled to our past."

The water shimmered beneath the sunset, and I felt movement inside of me. I recognized it as my heart racing.

"I'll never forget you," I whispered, "but I have to stop harboring the grief like it's all I've got left of you."

My voice cracked. "You were my first home, Low. But it's time to find a new place to put down roots. For me and Cam."

My words peacefully settled in the atmosphere. I felt serene as I realized the permission I sought could only be granted by me. I stood there a little while longer, relishing the wind pressing against my back. Like the gentlest nudge toward my future.

Then I turned, heading back down the trail. Alone, but full. Eager to experience whatever came next.

Chapter 29
Rudolph

I was baking beneath the relentless sun when the email hit, just after 11 a.m. The subject line, *Youth Empowerment Grant: Status Update*, was so ambiguous, it almost slipped past me. I thought there had been a delay in their decision. But as soon as I opened it and saw the word *approved*, my mouth went dry. We got it! *We*. But that word didn't sit right anymore.

Tawni wasn't here, or even a phone call away, to celebrate it with me. I wanted to congratulate her and tell her how proud I was of her. I pulled up her contact name in my phone and stared at it. But I couldn't bring myself to tap on it. Not yet. She'd given me space to figure out my shit, so I was doing the same for her. But I didn't know if that was even what she wanted.

The youth center was finally taking shape. They had framed walls, wiring, and plumbing, with flooring installed. Seeing tangible progress in the photos made me proud. I'd buried myself in this project and was finally able to see the fruit of my team's labor. Before the week ended, I took the entire crew out to dinner—on me. Not just to thank them for holding things down while I stepped back, but because I needed to acknowledge their effort out loud. Because it mattered. The vision couldn't have come to life without them, and they were more than a means to an end. They mattered to me.

They chose the restaurant, and after enjoying countless plates of wings and loaded fries, I pulled Chase aside.

"You've done an amazing job leading the team in my absence," I told him, patting him on the shoulder. "I owe you an apology. I treated you like an assistant when all this time, you were a leader. That's on me."

Chase shook his head, his expression finally relieved after all the tension we'd both been carrying. "I wasn't stepping up, Rue. Plain and simple. I just waited for you to tell me every move like I didn't know what I was doing. And that's on *me*."

"I know I can be intense," I admitted.

He smirked. "Now, if that isn't the understatement of the year."

"Right. But I see you," I continued, my eyes trained on him. "You've got this. And I trust you, Chase."

He nodded, dropping his head slightly. "I appreciate that, man. I never got a chance to share this with you, but you have a reputation for..."

I bristled, waiting for the hit.

"...being a badass in the construction world. When I learned I would be on your team, I wasn't only honored; I was pretty intimidated," he lowered his head again, running a hand through his blonde curls.

"I really look up to you. And I know I was letting you down. But when you went on leave, Glenn let us know how much this project meant to you. I knew this was my chance to step up. To prove I could do this."

He glanced back over at our table. "The whole team

stepped up. We all worked overtime to keep things on track. And Rue... I didn't have to beg one person to do it. They all wanted to."

I nodded, feeling that familiar sting in my eyes. *Don't you dare do it, Edwards.* I bit the inside of my cheek, then cleared my throat.

"Thanks, man," I said, then realized he needed more from me. "I didn't just trust you to run point while I was gone—I needed you to. And you owned it by keeping the momentum going without waiting on anyone's permission."

Chase looked down, almost sheepish, but I wasn't done.

"I've been holding on too tight, thinking if I didn't, the whole damn thing would collapse. But it didn't. I was able to breathe without looking over my shoulder." I exhaled slowly. "I've been burned before, man. People promising they'd show up and flaking the minute pressure hits. But that's no excuse because you aren't them, and you deserved better leadership from me."

His throat worked as he swallowed, and I could tell my words landed.

"You proved what you can do when you're properly poured into. You showed how much you care. I'll never forget that."

Chase blinked fast, then nodded. "Damn, I needed to hear that."

"I needed to say it just as much."

We lingered for a moment, realizing we hadn't always gotten it right but were finally getting somewhere that mattered. I hoped it would be a new beginning for both of us.

This morning, Cam, Brent, and I had taken the hour-long drive to Cedar Point. It was just the three of us hanging out for the day—laughing, eating overpriced burgers and funnel cake, and screaming like fools on the Valravn. It had been months since I'd fully let my guard down and enjoyed quality time with

Cameron, with no camp, schedules, or itineraries. On that day, the weight of expectation was gone. I was fully present, hands in the air, facing every metal beast the amusement park threw at us like we had something to prove.

While we were walking around the gift shop before heading home, Cam caught me watching him and elbowed me. "You're being all sentimental again."

I grinned. "Just taking it all in, bud."

"You're really happy, Dad. No filter needed," he said, picking up a Millennium Force tee.

"Yeah, Cam," I said, nodding and folding my arms across my chest. "I think I am."

* * *

That Friday, Chandler kept Cameron while I linked up with the crew. It was long overdue, and I knew I'd never hear the end of it. I walked in, excited for a night at Top Golf: good wings, bad jokes, and even worse swings.

Kenny lined up for his shot, narrowing his eyes like he was going for the championship title.

"Don't choke, my boy," Link called out just as Kenny pulled into his backswing. When Kenny broke form, Link leaned back in his chair with a smirk. "You been talkin' all night. Let's see some follow-through on that swing."

"I *live* in follow-through," Kenny shot back, readjusting his stance. "Unlike your fantasy football strategy."

Marcus nearly choked on his beer, laughing. "Come on now, Ken. Don't dump on him just because we all know his fantasy league's trash."

Dorian didn't even look up. "Y'all are overly loud. That's why your numbers are looking like this. Link's only beating you by two points, Kenny."

Link raised a brow. "So, you're *tracking* scores like we're at the Masters?"

Dorian shrugged. "Hey, if you can talk it, then walk it."

Marcus clapped his hands. "Man, this is exactly why we can only golf with each other. Y'all are unhinged. Straight embarrassing."

I shook my head and emptied my beer. I was strictly there for the laughs and the foolery, but the buzz barely cut through the static in my head.

Marcus slid into the booth next to me after his round. "You good, man? You been M.I.A. lately."

I forced a smile. "Yeah, I'm straight. Work's been wild."

Link raised an eyebrow. "That why you disappeared from the group chat *and* your relationship?"

Kenny chimed in, lowering his voice. "Nah, for real. We just wanna make sure you're not spiraling again, bruh. Last time you went silent on us, your brand new Xbox ended up on Craigslist."

I chuckled, but it didn't quite reach my chest. "I'm good, y'all. Just needed a little space for a minute. But I'm glad to be back like I never left."

"Them scores tellin' another story," Marcus cracked.

Dorian didn't comment. He was my private vault, who I knew I could trust with my secrets. But even around my closest friends, I felt like I was barely holding it together. The laughs rang a little too loud, the jokes bounced off me instead of ringing through me. My palms were sweating even in the AC, and a gnawing pit in my gut wouldn't ease up no matter how many times I wiped my hands on my shorts.

An hour in, I'd just sent one sailing toward the green when I heard, "Hey, you're Rue, right?"

I turned, squinting. A tall guy in a tailored pullover and

smart glasses walked up, extending his hand. "I'm Cedric. I work with Tawni."

My shoulders tensed at the mention of her, but Tawni had mentioned his name before. "Hey, man," I said, shaking his hand. "Nice to meet you."

"Same. She was telling me about the grant project and all the work you two put in. Congrats, I heard the funding came through."

News travels fast. I nodded. "Yeah. Just found out this week."

He smiled. "That's big. She's pretty proud, even if she doesn't say it."

I didn't know how to respond to that, so I didn't. My jaw clenched as I shoved my hands into the pockets of my shorts. My body went on autopilot, but my mind spiraled.

Thankfully, Cedric didn't linger. But he gave me a long look like he saw through the silence. He reminded me of my fifth-grade teacher, Mr. Spencer. "Give her a call, Rue," he said gently. "Sometimes too much time and space can quickly turn into a hostile standoff. She hasn't said it, but I know Tawni. She's waiting for you to step up to the plate. To choose her. Have a good evening."

I watched him walk off before sliding back into the booth, trying to play it cool. But the guys could read me better than a blueprint.

"That her boy or yours?" Kenny asked, half-joking.

"Tawni's coworker," I muttered.

Marcus leaned back. "Dude was familiar as fuck."

"Right?" Link said, leaning forward. "He was talking like he's known you for years."

"Unlike these guys, I respected your privacy. What'd he say?" Dorian asked, setting down his water.

I shrugged. "Told me I should call her."

"Are you?" Marcus asked.

I didn't answer.

Kenny chuckled. "Man, you overthink every damn thing. Call her, don't call her—just don't half-ass it. Women remember your effort, not whether the timing was perfect."

Something about that stuck with me. *Effort over perfect timing.*

I glanced out at the range; my thoughts were racing faster than I could process them. I could still hear Cedric's words like an echo in a tunnel. Tawni deserved to be chosen—not just included when it was convenient or comforted when I couldn't stand on my own. Calling her wouldn't be enough. She needed and expected much more from me.

I fished my phone out of my pocket without a word and opened my notes app. I started typing. Not just because I missed her or because Cedric had read me for filth in under two minutes. Because I now had a clear vision.

And the first step was vowing to never let fear lead my life again.

Chapter 30
Tawni

I hadn't seen Rue since popping up on him at the trailer. Not since he told me I wasn't his wife. I'd spent the morning smoothing every edge of myself, down to the pearl buttons on my pink blouse and the soft press of lip gloss. The moment I stepped into the meeting room, cool with air-conditioning and quiet chatter, my composure was already working overtime.

He was already seated at the table in a dark gray button-down and pressed slacks, freshly shaved. A small crease rested between his brows as I walked in and took a seat.

"Ms. Alexander," someone called brightly. A panelist with a clipboard and a warm smile. "Glad you could make it."

Rue stood and offered a courteous nod. "Good morning, Tawni."

My name on his lips struck a pressure point.

"Morning," I replied with a practiced smile. I took the empty seat beside him, careful not to let our elbows graze. His scent—cologne and fresh soap—invaded my nostrils, uninvited and unmistakable. It wrapped around me like a memory I wasn't ready to relive, flooding my chest before I could block it out, pulling at the soft and stupid parts inside of me. My breath caught before I could check it, and I forced myself to focus on anything but the way my body remembered his.

Thankfully, the grant selection panel began introducing themselves one by one. There was a representative from the Cleveland Youth Resilience Grant, two program officers from the Wilson Foundation, a youth development liaison from the Department of Education, and a communications director from the Greater Cleveland Youth Network. Each seemed ready to decide if our program would make it to the finish line—or not.

Sylvia, from the Wilson Foundation, all sharp cheekbones and burgundy lipstick, folded her hands in front of her. "Thanks for joining us today. Let's begin with the inspiration behind your proposal. What motivated you to develop these enrichment programs?"

Rue looked at me, and I gave him a brief smile. Then we did what we always did when it came to our passion for the youth—we aligned.

"The target community is filled with brilliant, underserved teens who are often overlooked," I said, my voice steady. "Rue and I each have seen firsthand how powerful mentorship, creative programming, and access to opportunity can be when young people are met where they are."

Rue nodded, picking up the thread without missing a beat. "Many of the kids in this community are carrying adult-sized burdens. With a space that's safe and empowering, they can focus on developing their voices in a nurturing environment and learn how to immediately use them to build future career plans."

We volleyed back and forth, answering questions for over thirty minutes—finishing each other's thoughts, bridging each other's gaps, and falling back into our natural rhythm. But thick tension still sat in the space between our chairs, refusing to budge. Every time his hand moved to gesture, my body stiffened, hoping it wouldn't graze mine. It never did.

When a panelist asked about our working dynamic, I caught the flicker of apprehension in Rue's eyes before he spoke. "I'll be designing the construction management curriculum, and Tawni will take the lead on the youth-centered initiative," he said evenly. "We have a mutual respect for what the other brings to the table. She's a brilliant strategist an advocate heart, and I fully trust her to direct these programs. Her work ethic speaks for itself."

I swallowed hard and folded my hands in my lap before speaking. "Rue's insight and experience are what gave this vision its roots. His devotion to the community is unmatched. His ties to community leaders will open up partnering opportunities for career talks, classroom activities, and sponsored events."

The words came out smooth, polished, professional because I believed them. But my ribs still trembled with each breath.

The final question came from the youngest panelist, a man who looked like he was barely out of grad school.

"What do you want the youth take away from your program?"

Silence fell over us.

Then Rue spoke quietly. "The feeling that they're not alone. That who they are today—however complicated or unsure—is all they need to be successful."

I glanced at him, knowing this wasn't just words for him. The passion in his voice was evident. My throat tightened as my emotions threatened to consume me. After a beat, I added, "My hope is for their realization that their stories are worth telling. That healing and growth are possible when you're allowed to be just who you are and feel nurtured, valued, and respected. It takes a village, and we're ready to stand in the gap societal systems have left behind in order to cheer them on."

A short pause followed as a couple of panelists jotted down notes. Another gave a small nod and smile. When the interview ended, we shook hands, thanked them, and left the room. Rue stood beside me with his hands in his pockets, waiting for the hallway to clear. Soon, we were alone.

"I just want to say you did a phenomenal job in there," he said softly. His eyes were trained on me. "You were in your element and I meant every word I said."

I nodded numbly. "So were you and so did I."

A long pause stretched between us, but I didn't break the silence because I didn't have anything else to say.

He rubbed the back of his neck. "I wasn't sure how this would go for us. I almost wanted to ask to do it solo."

I raised an eyebrow. "You wanted to pitch a two-person initiative alone?"

He gave a half-hearted smile. "I didn't say it was a *good* idea."

I scoffed, wanting to laugh and cry. Instead, I adjusted the strap on my bag.

"Well, I'm glad we didn't," I said. "They needed to see us both."

Rue nodded, then looked away. "Yeah."

I turned to leave, but not before catching the pain in his eyes when he looked at me. He seemed tortured, like he wanted to say something else but didn't trust himself. Although that ache was mirrored inside of me, but I walked away without another word.

Some gaps couldn't be bridged with words alone. And neither of us was quite ready to meet the other halfway.

* * *

The makeshift dressing room at Cherry's was barely big enough for a coat rack and a mirror, but that didn't stop my village from squeezing in with hugs, lip gloss, affirmations, and well wishes.

"Somebody pass me the safety pins," Trish said, holding up the hem of my top like we weren't less than ten minutes from showtime.

"I still think you should've gone with the burgundy dress. Here, sip some more of this," Jaclyn said, handing me my mug of green tea.

I side-eyed her. Girl just couldn't help herself.

"Be quiet," Mom said, waving her off. "She looks stunning." She smoothed the back of my hair down while studying my reflection in the mirror in front of us.

Tiff knelt beside me, adjusting the strap on my stiletto. "Your voice is the only thing that matters tonight. Everything else is just extra."

Just then, Cedric popped his head in, grinning. "Hey, there's our superstar. You're gonna kill it."

Unable to turn around, I smiled at his reflection and blew him a kiss in the mirror. Ms. Karr walked up behind him, followed by Hannah with a huge bouquet of sunflowers. They all took their turns shuffling in and out of the room in brief shifts, giving me hugs and kisses.

"Okay, y'all. T. Lexx needs a moment to breathe before she hits the stage," Tiff announced. "We're asking that you please clear out unless you're blood, besties, or backup vocals."

Everyone began to shuffle out, and Tip, the stage manager, walked in with a massive bouquet of white gold-tipped tulips, yellow gold-tipped garden roses, and lavender sprigs, all wrapped in deep gold tissue and tied with a ribbon.

"Another bouquet?" I asked, struggling to hold the large arrangement. "Y'all are going over the top tonight."

Everyone glanced at each other, confused.

Tiff frowned. "They're beautiful, but we didn't send them."

Trish shrugged and gestured toward the corner. "We chipped in on the dozen roses. Even collectively, we couldn't bankroll something like this."

Jaclyn leaned over to peek at the tiny card tucked inside. "There's no name. It just says, 'You deserve each standing ovation you'll receive tonight.'"

I examined them closely, taking in their scent with a deep inhale as I set them gently on the counter. Someone knew the color palette of my outfit and how much tonight mattered to me. I had a pretty strong feeling who it was, but I had to push that out of my mind. I needed a clear head before hitting the stage. "Okay... well, I'll just add this mystery bouquet to my little corner of inspiration."

I handed the flowers to Trish and forced my trembling hands to still as they smoothed out my dress. Mom whispered a prayer over me, and Jaclyn pressed her forehead to mine, just like we did when we were kids. It was a powerful moment, reminding me how far we'd allowed ourselves to come.

A few moments later, I was alone, doing my breathing and vocal exercises. The tea mug trembled in my tight grip. My nerves were doing me dirty. I chose to focus on the meaning behind my lyrics and the years of dreaming and hard work that led to this moment. Soon, the lights began to flicker, and I could barely feel my legs as I walked down the corridor, giving the stage crew and staff high-fives as I prepared to step onto the stage.

Under the powerful overhead lights, the crowd morphed into a blurred mass of heads and camera flashes. But my eyes found him right away. He was standing off to the side with his arms crossed, trying to blend in. But he could never fade into a crowd. My heart had clocked him before my eyes did.

He came. Even after weeks of silence and the letter. But by the time I made it through the final verse of *Under October Moonlight,* I scanned the room again—and he was gone. My chest tightened, but I kept smiling as I serenaded the crowd through the final hook. Because this was my moment. My album release that I'd worked on for years. His presence—no matter how brief—had meant the world to me, but this wasn't about him.

I stepped offstage to a prolonged wave of claps, cheers, and a group of people holding out flyers and hugging my neck like I'd just dropped a platinum album instead of a debut EP.

Tiff pulled me aside and introduced me to DJ Luxx, who'd done a phenomenal job emceeing the event. "You sounded so good tonight," she told me. "I heard your demo last year, but it doesn't do you any justice. You've definitely leveled up, sis. You've got pipes, and live performances are where you excel. When I saw you perform at the music festival, I knew you were someone I needed to meet," she said with a wink. "I've also stopped by a few of your recent shows, and you didn't disappoint."

I wanted to scream with excitement, but instead, I pressed my palms together and placed them on my chest. "Thanks, Luxx. I always feed off of the crowd's energy, and they definitely brought it this evening."

"Here's my direct number," she said, handing me a glossy pink business card. "Give me a call so we can schedule a live radio interview ASAP. I'd also like to recommend you for the summer jam next year. You know how to rock a crowd, and that's exactly what we need for our local talent segment."

"That sounds amazing," I said. "I'll definitely be in touch with you soon. Thanks again for hosting."

Stunned, I turned to face Tiff, who grinned like a proud mama. "You've officially reached star status, sis. Don't forget you're A-1 day ones now that you've blown up."

Smiling, I waved her off. "Girl, hardly. Singing is just a hobby for now. My heart lies in teaching and mentoring."

"Yeah, okay. But if you need a manager once your single blows up, all I need is enough time to put in my two weeks' notice," she joked, chucking the deuces.

"You're a fool," I said, snatching the marker from her.

Still breathless from the high of it all, I turned to the crowd awaiting me. I signed my name on flyers, hugged friends from work, and posed for dozens of pictures in front of the step-and-repeat Jaclyn designed for me.

"You killed it, work bestie," Cedric said, giving me a firm nod as he passed by. "Spotify better get ready."

"And that's facts," I said.

My heart was still racing as my adrenaline shot into overdrive. But my mind kept looping back to Rue. He'd been standing near the back, half-shadowed by the lights. But I knew I saw him. Somewhere between the third and fourth song, when I was fully in my element, he must have slipped out. And now he was gone.

Still, I smiled, keeping it together for the people who stayed. I was surrounded by love and support. I was finally realizing everything I'd dreamed about for years.

When a woman stepped forward, holding one of the promo flyers close to her chest, I smiled at her.

"T. Lexx, could you sign this for me?" she asked softly.

"Of course," I said, reaching for it. "Who should I make it out to?"

She smiled. "Farrah Stephens."

My head snapped up, my eyes searching her face in disbelief. Her eyes squinted in the corners in that familiar way. She looked almost exactly like the last memory I had of her—eyes bright, full of knowing. A little older, but still her. Still *my* Farrah.

"Oh my God. Is it you?" I whispered, covering my mouth.

She nodded, tears already welling up. "It's me, Tawni."

I dropped the marker and pulled her into a hug, nearly knocking the wind out of both of us. We didn't speak at first—just clung to each other, sobbing and giggling like schoolgirls transported back in time.

"I can't believe it's you," I whispered into her hair.

"Me either! It's so good to see you," she said, pulling back, smiling at me through her tears.

"Wait, you understand me without reading my lips?" I asked, frowning.

Her smile widened. "Yes. My dad found a surgeon who restored my hearing during middle school."

I gasped, and for a moment, I couldn't find my voice.

All these years, I'd held on to this image of Farrah as the sweet, soft-spoken Deaf girl, frozen in time. I'd wrapped her in a narrative of fragility and loss—someone I had to protect. But she wasn't that girl anymore and hadn't been for a long time. She'd moved on, grown, and lived a life I'd never even imagined for her. My heart swelled with awe. Here she was, full of joy, strength, and living life to her own soundtrack. I could barely wrap my head around it.

"I still love signing," she continued, "but I completely fell in love with music. Of course, T. Lexx is my new favorite artist!"

I laughed, still staring at her like she could disappear at any moment.

"And girl, your voice..." Her eyes softened. "Rich, bold, and full of energy. Hearing it for the first time somehow brought me right back to our precious elementary school days."

We shared another tight squeeze before catching up in a

rush of overlapping questions and memories for the next fifteen minutes.

Then I asked, "So how did you find my music? My YouTube channel?"

"No, your friend reached out. I still can't believe he found me."

I blinked. "Who, Cedric?"

She shook her head. "He said his name was Rudolph. He DM'd a private Instagram account I barely use. When he told me about your music and the showcase, coming tonight wasn't even a second thought. I live in Indiana now, but he said it would mean a lot for you to see me. So I drove up last night."

Her lips were still moving after that, but I couldn't keep up with much of what she said. After his silence for the past several weeks, Rue's actions spoke for him: reconnecting me with a long-lost friend I never thought I'd see again. I didn't know what to think or how to feel. I was still confused by him leaving the show early, giving me the gorgeous flowers, and this thoughtful gesture. But I was certain of one thing. I owed him a thank you and the chance to be heard.

Chapter 31
Tawni

After an unprecedented heatwave that lasted over a week, I was grateful for the opportunity to leave my house before sunset again. Rue had asked me to meet him in downtown Chagrin Falls, so I parked and walked over to a row of shops wearing a denim skirt and cutoff tank top. I usually dressed up whenever I saw him, but it had been a casual day of cleaning while streaming my songs on Spotify.

I approached him slowly, curious to see him holding ice cream cones.

"What is this, a vanilla bean peace offering?" I asked dryly, biting back my giddiness.

"You know it," he said, cracking a cautious smile as he handed it over.

We walked for a few blocks without saying much at first, weaving past retail shops and admiring flower boxes. We reached a shaded bench and took a seat facing a row of restaurants.

He sat down and let a few moments pass before saying,

"Congratulations on winning the grant for your workshops. I'm excited to see it all come to fruition for you."

I nodded. "Thanks. I couldn't have done it without your support through the whole process."

"It was the least I could do. I'd like to introduce you to my friend Sidney. He's going to be the director of a leadership development program for first-generation students at a sister youth center," he said, wiping his hand on a napkin. "You two should definitely link."

"I'd love that," I said.

A few moments passed, but it wasn't the easy silence I'd grown accustomed to. For the first time, things felt awkward between us.

I cleared my throat. "I also want to thank you for reconnecting me with Farrah. Seeing her at my showcase meant the world to me."

"Yeah, finding her wasn't easy. But Sidney's girlfriend, Aubri, was able to track her down. Farrah was happy to hear that you'd pursued singing. She said you would always sing along to BET videos at your sleepovers."

I laughed. "Wow, I can't believe she still remembers that," I said, licking the edge of my cone to catch the fast-melting ice cream.

Rue stared at me for a second, and I stopped, mid-lick. "Probably wasn't the best idea to get ice cream today... or maybe it was."

I rolled my eyes at his arched brow. "Cedric said he saw you at Top Golf the other week."

He nodded. "Yeah, he pretty much gave his two cents and dipped."

"Sounds like Ced. He's got it honest for sure. Hopefully, he didn't offend you."

"No, he didn't overstep. But I could tell how much he cares

about you," he said.

"We've been through a lot together," I said, swatting a bee eyeing my cone. "Fighting for your students doesn't get you many popularity points. So we have each other's backs."

He nodded again. "I'm sure that's true."

Rue cleared his throat and turned his body to face me. "So, the voice memo, Tawni..."

I bristled at his abrupt subject change. But I could understand why he wanted to get it off his chest.

"... obviously, that wasn't for you. And I'm sorry. That message... it wasn't fair to you."

He exhaled and glanced away. "I didn't realize the impact until I listened to it myself. Hearing your name come out of my mouth in a message meant for her... made me realize how much of my present I was still filtering through the past."

He rubbed the back of his neck. "I don't want to keep doing that."

I sat still, watching him squirm, wanting badly to step in and save him, but needing to hear his full truth.

"I miss her," he said, exhaling. "That's the truth. But that doesn't mean I can't make space for someone else. For you. And the way I hurt you... I just hate that I did that."

I nodded slowly. "I'd never ask you to forget her, Rue. I just... I need to know I'm not just a fill-in for her."

His brows pulled together, and he shook his head. "You're not. You never were."

He leaned back against the bench, drumming his fingers against his thigh. "I didn't handle anything right. I lashed out. I shut down. Said shit that I deeply regret."

I gave him a long look. "You did."

His eyes searched mine, and I could tell he was unsure if he should keep going.

"But you're here now," I added. "And that counts for something."

Rue looked away, the side of his mouth twitching like he wanted to say something else but couldn't find the words.

He looked at the ground. "I didn't realize I was still clinging on to her. Using her voice in my head to help with making critical parenting decisions that I wasn't sure about. It just made me feel like my wife and best friend was still there to help guide me. But along the way, I now realize that I stopped trusting myself."

I let his words settle for a minute before I spoke. "I want you to know that I would never ask you to forget Willow, Rue. I was there for a small part of that loss, and I could see how deep it impacted you and Cameron."

He nodded with his eyes trained on me.

"But I can't be the emotional bridge for the person you're still asking for permission. I need room to be loved in full. And if you're not ready for that, I respect it. There will always be space for Willow in you and Cameron's hearts, and that's beautiful. But I need to be loved for who I am, not for how I can soothe the absence of someone else in your life."

He tossed his long-forgotten cone in the trash can beside him. "You would never have to."

"I have doubts," I admitted. "I wonder if you see her in the back of your mind when you're with me."

His expression morphed into confusion. "Not even for a moment. Tawni, she was my partner and my best friend. But I've started learning how to lean on *me*. Trusting my people. And you. I want to stop surviving and start living again. I want to move forward. And I want you in that future."

I swallowed. That, more than anything else he could've said, landed.

"I also started going back to therapy, and she helped me

realize how drowning myself in work and failing to rely on my team was impacting me," he said. "I've created a new workflow that delegates a third of my project management tasks to Chase, my project coordinator. It's a small step in the right direction."

I nodded, clasping my hands. These were all positive things to hear, but I wanted to be sure it wasn't just lip service. "What about Cam?"

"We talked," Rue said softly. "I told him what you mean to me. And he said he remembered how safe Willow made him feel. You remind him of that."

Tears burned behind my eyes. "He really said that?"

"He did. Tawni, I'd never let you shrink to fit in my life," Rue said. "I want you in it. Fully as yourself. I'd walk away before trying to force you to live in another woman's shadow."

I didn't know what else to say, so I bit into my waffle cone. He watched me stress-eat the rest of it in silence. Then he held out a hand for my balled-up napkin.

We stayed quiet for a bit longer.

"Okay, there's something I need to tell you," I said, glancing down at my lap. "It's about my previous relationship with Dante."

Rue nodded and turned his body to fully face me but remained silent, listening.

"When we were together, I tried to keep the peace as much as I could. He was blunt and outspoken, so I often let his disrespectful behavior slide. He'd say and do things that never should've been excused. With each incident I overlooked, I lost a piece of myself. And by the time I realized how much I'd shrunk to make room for his bullshit, I no longer recognized myself."

I looked up, meeting Rue's eyes.

"So when things got serious with you and I started to feel

that way again, it triggered me. Because I promised myself I'd never settle for anyone who didn't accept *all* of me."

Rue nodded slowly. "You deserve all of that. From me."

"And from myself," I added. "But thank you. For hearing me."

He reached for my hand, brushing his thumb across the back of it. "Now that you've explained your need for keeping the peace, I understand things a little better. At first, I think I was seeking your feedback regarding Cam. Asking you for advice because you know him. I was asking you to fill a space that you weren't ready for yet. I'll admit, I was a little frustrated when you redirected me back to trusting my own decisions."

I nodded, remembering our conversation in Akron.

"But now I not only respect your decision to stand firm on your boundary; I'm grateful for it. If you'd chosen to provide parenting advice, I would have just been replacing my dependency on Willow with relying on you," he said, continuing to stroke my hand. "I needed to stand on my own and begin to trust myself. I'm a great father who's a work in progress when it comes to navigating parenthood. And..."

"*—that's okay,*" we said together in my elementary school teacher voice.

We shared a laugh, both of us realizing how much I was rubbing off on him.

"I'm sorry it took me so long to be ready for you," he said. "I never wanted you to dim your light just because I was stuck in my own shadow."

I smiled, a little sad for all he'd gone through. But I was also grateful. "Like you've so graciously told me before, you're worth it."

We shared a chuckle.

"And... thank you for bringing Farrah back into my life. I

never thought I'd be able to receive that kind of healing. But you knew."

He shrugged. "She was such an important part of your story. You just deserved the chance to reconnect with her and let her know what she still means to you."

"I did," I said, placing my hand on my chest. "Seeing her thriving and living her life on her own terms meant everything to me."

"I'm glad," he said, squeezing my hand.

We sat in silence for a few moments, enjoying the buzzing activity around us.

Rue looked down at our joined hands for a moment, then released a soft breath. "There's one more thing I haven't shared with you yet. And you deserve to know."

I gave him my full attention, sensing the shift in his tone.

"I have anxiety," he said plainly, but I could tell the words carried weight for him. "I've had it since childhood, but I didn't always name it. I spent a lot of time thinking I could outrun it. Or bury it in work."

He paused, searching my face for a reaction. I nodded for him to continue.

"My doctor recently increased my dosage, and I've been feeling much better. I admit, I wasn't taking it consistently when everything started falling apart. When you showed up at the trailer that day, I was in the thick of it. Burnt out, running on fumes, and drowning in pressure I didn't know how to hold anymore."

My heart broke for him, but I realized how important it was for me to keep a strong front for him. I held his gaze and nodded.

"I'm not sharing any of that as an excuse," he added quickly. "But you didn't deserve to walk into that storm, Tawni.

I didn't handle myself well at all. I scared you and hurt you. I shut you out. And I'm... really, truly sorry for all of it."

"I appreciate that. Thanks, Rue," I said, gently squeezing his hand and giving him room to continue.

"I knew something had to change. So I took a voluntary leave for two weeks. This is the first time I've done anything like that. Stopping cold and focusing on getting back to myself instead of just pushing through the pain. Resting. Getting consistent with my meds again. Rebuilding routines that support me, not drain me... asking for help."

He looked at me, eyes open and vulnerable. "I'm serious about being better. Not just for you. For myself, for Cam, and for the kind of life I want to live."

I blinked, emotion rising in my throat. "Thanks for sharing that with me. That means a lot, Rue. Truly."

He looked relieved, but caution still lingered in his eyes.

Sighing, I said, "You made your mental health a priority. That takes bravery, self-awareness, and follow-through. And you're not alone in this journey, Rue. You never were. I'm right here with you," I added, letting my thumb sweep gently across his. "However you need me."

His chest rose with a deep breath, and he nodded. "I wasn't sure you'd still want to be."

I gave him a soft smile. "I never stopped wanting to. I just needed you to meet me where I was. And now... here we are."

He nodded and leaned in for a quick peck on the lips. I didn't pull back, realizing how much I missed him.

I smiled at him, choosing my next words carefully. "Rue, there's nothing I want more than to continue this with you. You and Cameron have held a special place in my heart ever since I first met you."

He reached over and squeezed my hand. "I want this, too."

"But," I continued, "it has to be different. We have to

always lead with honesty. And most importantly, be present with each other."

Rue nodded. "Of course. We'll ease back into it. I'm gonna enjoy earning back every bit of your trust. But..."

I frowned. "But what?"

"I need you to work on being more open with me," he said. "Sometimes, opening up to you can be difficult because you can be walled off. No one says everything they're thinking, but if we're going to get to know each other better, I need to know what you're thinking, Tawn."

I nodded. "That's fair. My friends often tell me the same thing. I try to avoid conflict, but I see how it's impacting my relationships."

"That's understandable. But all conflict isn't bad."

"I promise to work on letting you know when things upset me. You deserve to know what's going on with me. And..." I said, taking a deep breath. "Now that I understand some of the challenges you've had with single parenting, I'd be happy to offer my opinion about important matters that concern Cameron. But if you ever feel like I'm over-stepping..."

"I'll definitely let you know. But honestly, I've never had a reason to question your intentions with Cam."

My cheeks flushed. There was no sweeping romantic moment needed when it came to reconciliation between us. We were just two people trying again, and it felt great because that had always been enough for me. I exhaled, finally feeling a release. This was exactly where I wanted to be. Where we each deserved to be.

We stood and walked over to the nearby waterfall, its droplets catching the sunlight just right. Rue wrapped his arms around me and pulled me close. We shared several long kisses as the the cool mist coated our skin.

Then he pulled out his phone, excitement dancing in his eyes.

"What are you doing," I asked.

"I'm thinking we should document our reboot."

"Oh, absolutely," I said, leaning into his chest.

He bent down to fit in the frame, and our heads touched. Warmth spread through my chest. It felt amazing to be in his strong arms again. Our giddy smiles modeled our eagerness to begin again as he snapped each photo. Holding hands, we turned to head toward the parking lot. Something real, fragile, and sacred was blooming between us.

We had a ways to go, but a soft reboot and a promising new beginning were a good start. Because this time, I was excited to write a story that would be all ours.

Epilogue

Tawni: Four Months Later

The grand opening was just days away, and the energy around the youth center felt like the start of something groundbreaking. We weren't aiming for anything loud or flashy—just an intentional connection with the community. Rue and I planned each part of the curriculum together, like we were placing a final stone in place on a project built with love.

I stood near the front entrance of the student enrichment center, watching Rue quietly supervise the signage team as they secured the brushed steel letters to the interior walkway. His generous donation had allowed him to name a small section, which would be known as the construction management program: *The Willow Construction Management Program.* Even from a few feet away, I could feel how the moment anchored him and Cameron as the sign was affixed to the wall.

As they silently stared at it, I slid my hand into Rue's and gave it a gentle squeeze. "I'm sure she'd be proud. I hope you are, too."

He nodded, slowly. "I am. This place will be a second chance for a lot of kids. Maybe even for me."

That part made me smile. Rue had spent the last few months pouring himself into designing the construction management program to be a mentoring opportunity for students. Rigorous workshops would be led by members of his network of architects and project managers. Cameron even helped create the welcome kiosk with his robotics club. The impact would touch kids and change their whole trajectory.

A few days ago, we honored Willow's birthday on the beach. Just the three of us. I made her favorite—strawberry crunch cake. As the sun set, Cameron lit the first sky lantern and whispered, "Gone but never forgotten. We love you, Mom." We stood there for a while, watching them float into the night sky, each of us silently sending up our own version of gratitude for the impact she made on the lives of the guys standing beside me.

Rue and Willow were born a day apart, so I threw him a surprise party the following evening with the theme Chucks, Cigars & Champagne. The Sneaker Ball was held at a rooftop ballroom overlooking the lake. The invitation read, *"Suited & Sneakered—Celebrate in Style,"* and his friends and family came dressed to impress.

The space sparkled with candlelight and gold accents, with a sea of tailored suit jackets, sequin gowns, and fresh kicks that deserved their own red carpet. I brought in a live saxophonist, supplied a cigar bar on the terrace, and top-shelf champagne flowed all night.

I'd told Rue we were going to a fundraising gala. He walked in stunned, wearing a deep navy tux and crisp white Chucks that I had custom-embroidered with the words *"Built for This"* on the soles. He froze, scanning the cheering crowd of his loved ones for a second, taking it all in.

I leaned in and asked, "Do you see all the people who showed up tonight, just for you?"

He nodded.

"These are the people you've had all along."

His eyes welled up right before the toast, but when he spoke, his voice was steady.

"This isn't just a party," he said, holding up a flute. "It's proof that joy still lives here. Right, Killa Cam?" He crossed his arms over his chest in an X, then thumped it. I spotted Cameron in the crowd, nodding and doing the same. Then Rue turned to face me. "And to the woman who made it all possible. Tawni, thanks for being my rock. Your devotion to me and Cameron is unmatched. I love you."

I gasped, lowering my glass before it slipped from my hand. Hearing those three words for the first time in front of all his family and friends—Willow's family—almost took my breath away. He gave a slight nod, affirming he meant every word.

"I can't think of anyone who deserves this more. I love you, too," I said, blinking back tears.

He leaned down to kiss me, and the room erupted in applause. We danced, laughed, and toasted to fresh starts. Rue was surrounded by love, legacy, and people who'd shown up for him through all the hard parts and stayed to help him celebrate the good ones.

Today was also special, but for a different reason. It was our first official family outing for Rue, Cameron, and me. We were hanging out at their house when Cameron suggested that we hit up Fun 'N' Stuff. We raced go-karts, played several rounds of putt-putt, enjoyed the indoor rides, and battled each other in multiple rounds of laser tag.

Rue and I sat on a bench near the snack bar, sharing soft pretzels and slushies while Cameron was on the skating rink.

"I didn't know it could feel this easy," he said, brushing a salt flake off my lip.

I smiled. "I did. But only with you."

He grinned like a shy schoolboy. "Where do you see this going, Ms. Alexander?"

I looked past him for a second. Cameron had narrowly escaped a collision with a cluster of backward-skating teenage girls. When he emerged unscathed, I turned back to Rue.

"Hmm, I see late-night ice cream runs and early-morning school drop-offs. Chess conventions, community projects, and maybe a summer house with a porch swing one day. I see a timeless love that doesn't need to compete with anything else—one that makes room for everything. And," I said, kissing him on the lips, "most importantly, I see you choosing me every single day on purpose. Right after I choose you."

Rue gave me that slow smile that I'd come to adore. "I see all that, too. And I do see you being my wife one day."

I fought off a squeal as I returned his smile and said, "Well, that's a vision I can fully support, Mr. Edwards."

Cameron came racing back, waving a flyer in the air. "They have VR bowling! Let's go!"

Rue stood and reached for my hand. "Come on, babe. Looks like our break is over."

Placing my hand in his, I smiled, knowing this was just the beginning of everything we'd been brave enough to hope for. We all walked into the arcade, laughing and joking with the neon lights flashing all around us. That's when I felt it—that spark that had finally returned to my life. Passion, purpose, and fulfillment. I didn't have to chase them anymore because I'd attracted them.

Rue and I were finally in tune—two hearts playing a melody in the same key. Love in the key of summer.

Acknowledgments

I'm incredibly thankful for the people who continue to read my books, send emails, and share my work with others. May you continue to find value in the stories I share.

To my husband, Doug, thanks for listening to me think out loud while planning my stories. You're incredible.

To the other thirds of the Lit Trio, Michael C. Payne and JJ Winston, thanks for your continued support of my author journey. It's great to have each of you as my writing besties. May our characters live on in each other's stories.

To you, my reader, I hope you enjoyed reading about Tawni and Rue. I love hearing from you, so please visit my website at www.zariahlbanks.com, read a blog or two, and sign up for my email list to stay in touch.

Until our next chapter,
Z

About the Author

Zariah L. Banks is an award-winning contemporary romance author. Beauty Beheld was a featured title in the Indie Author Project Select collection, one of the best indie books in the Indie Author Project program on Biblioboard.

Zariah *loves* book clubs! As an avid book club member for most of her adult life, she would love a personal invite to attend yours. For a free Book Club Discussion Guide complete with an appetizer menu and relationship Q&A's, or to request an author appearance for your book club discussion, please fill out a book club request form at www.ZariahLBanks.com/bookclubbae. Zariah is available to attend book club meetings as a virtual guest.

Connect with Zariah on social media!